Murder at
Waters Edge
by

Kathi Daley

I want to thank the very talented Jessica Fischer for the cover art.

I so appreciate Bruce Curran, who is always ready and willing to answer my cyber questions, and Peggy Hyndman for helping sleuth out those pesky typos.

And, of course, thanks to the readers and bloggers in my life, who make doing what I do possible.

Thank you to Randy Ladenheim-Gil for the editing.

Special thanks to Connie Correll, Martie Peck, Vivian Shane, and Elizabeth Dent for submitting recipes.

And finally I want to thank my sister Christy for always lending an ear and my husband Ken for allowing me time to write by taking care of everything else.

Books by Kathi Daley

Come for the murder, stay
for the romance.

Zoe Donovan Cozy Mystery:

Halloween Hijinks
The Trouble With Turkeys
Christmas Crazy
Cupid's Curse
Big Bunny Bump-off
Beach Blanket Barbie
Maui Madness
Derby Divas
Haunted Hamlet
Turkeys, Tuxes, and Tabbies
Christmas Cozy
Alaskan Alliance
Matrimony Meltdown
Soul Surrender
Heavenly Honeymoon
Hopscotch Homicide
Ghostly Graveyard
Santa Sleuth
Shamrock Shenanigans
Kitten Kaboodle
Costume Catastrophe

Candy Cane Caper
Holiday Hangover
Easter Escapade
Camp Carter – *July 2017*

Zimmerman Academy The New Normal
Ashton Falls Cozy Cookbook

Whales and Tails Cozy Mystery:
Romeow and Juliet
The Mad Catter
Grimm's Furry Tail
Much Ado About Felines
Legend of Tabby Hollow
Cat of Christmas Past
A Tale of Two Tabbies
The Great Catsby
Count Catula
The Cat of Christmas Present
A Winter's Tail
The Taming of the Tabby – *June 2017*

Seacliff High Mystery:
The Secret
The Curse
The Relic
The Conspiracy
The Grudge
The Shadow – *June 2017*

Sand and Sea Hawaiian Mystery:
Murder at Dolphin Bay
Murder at Sunrise Beach
Murder at the Witching Hour
Murder at Christmas
Murder at Turtle Cove
Murder at Waters Edge

Road to Christmas Romance:
Road to Christmas Past

Writer's Retreat Southern Mystery:
First Case
Second Look – *July 2017*

Tj Jensen Paradise Lake Mysteries by Henery Press
Pumpkins in Paradise
Snowmen in Paradise
Bikinis in Paradise
Christmas in Paradise
Puppies in Paradise
Halloween in Paradise

Treasure in Paradise
Fireworks in Paradise – *October 2017*

Note to Readers

As of the date this book will be published, several of the locations mentioned are closed due to flooding. It's uncertain when they'll reopen so please be sure to check ahead of time if you're planning a trip to Maui and are considering a visit to any of the places mentioned in the story.

Chapter 1

Saturday, April 29

"For those of you who are just joining us, I want to welcome you to the halfway point of the final leg of the Amazing Brains and Brawn Race for one—million—dollars," a portly man in a red-and-white Hawaiian shirt said to the crowd. He spoke through a megaphone that not only amplified his voice but added to the air of anticipation as he paused between each word when announcing the amount of the grand prize. "As those of you who have been following this event know, a hundred teams entered the contest four weeks ago. During those four weeks, the teams with the lowest scores have been eliminated and now all that remain are the top-ten teams. Today is the halfway point of the finals, so we're taking a break to enable the contestants to regroup before making the push to the finish line. The teams with the lowest scores will be eliminated every day from this point forward. The final two teams in the running at the end of the week will compete next Saturday for all that money. The winner will be announced on Sunday, May 7."

I tried to pay attention to the announcer, who I was certain would say something I'd end up wishing I'd paid more attention to, but all I could think of was conspiracy and death. My name is Kailani Pope, although everyone except my paternal grandmother calls me Lani. I'm a resident of Oahu but am currently on leave from my job as a water safety officer for the Dolphin Bay Resort to participate in the Amazing Brains and Brawn Race being held on Maui. Participating in the event isn't something I've always aspired to and most likely never would have entered; I was there as a substitute for the sister of my good friend Bethany Halderman, who'd called me on Thursday night to tell me her sister Cammy, a contestant, had been killed in a terrible accident earlier in the evening. According to Bethany, Cammy had called her the morning before her broken body was found at the bottom of a cliff near the resort where the people competing for the million dollars were staying. Cammy had shared with Bethany her suspicion that there was more going on with the hacks the contestants were being asked to complete each day than met the eye. Bethany believed her sister, who was very bright and a computer geek, had discovered something someone didn't want revealed. This, she reasoned, was the real impetus for Cammy's *accidental* tumble from the cliff onto the rocks below, rather than the excess alcohol her teetotalling sister supposedly had drunk.

Bethany and I decided I would enter the competition as Cammy's replacement. This would allow me to snoop around from the inside and hopefully find out what really had happened to Cammy. The rules provided for the selection of replacements should one or more of the contestants be unable to continue due to major injury or death. Cammy's team partner, Stone Silverman, had also been her fiancé. He, understandably, had been so devastated by her death that he'd dropped out and returned home to the mainland. That left Cammy's team still missing a player and with an additional problem. Those of you who know me are aware that although I'm only five feet tall, I'm fit and strong and can most likely handle the brawn part of any team, but the brains part—the part where you hack your way into a website to obtain the first clue of the day—is just a bit out of my wheelhouse.

My boyfriend, Luke Austin, was pretty good with a computer. Unfortunately, he was in Texas, meeting his brand-new niece. Cammy's body was found on Thursday evening, after she had completed her tasks for the day, and today was Saturday, so I'd already missed any points Team Honu—the name Stone and Cammy had come up with—would have received from competing yesterday. Fortunately, today, day seven of the fourteen-day finals, was a day of rest, so as long as I could compete tomorrow, when the eliminations began, I should be good to go.

I needed brains to go with my brawn and I needed them fast. Initially I'd had no idea where I was going to come up with someone on such short notice; then I'd remembered my new friend, superhacker and software magnet Zak Zimmerman. Zak was one of the best hackers in the world, so I'd asked him and his wife, Zoe, if they'd be willing to come to Maui for a week to help me uncover a conspiracy. Zoe, who's even more into sleuthing than I am, promised to be on the next plane west. Actually, they were arriving by private plane, but I got the idea.

"Excuse me," I said to a tall woman with long dark hair who was sitting at one of the booths that had been set up to answer whatever questions the contestants had as they headed into the final week. "My name is Kailani Pope. I'm the replacement for Cammy Halderman."

The woman looked at me with soft eyes. "I heard about what happened. I spoke to Cammy on several occasions. She was such a sweet little thing. Her accident was such a tragedy. Were you and Cammy friends?"

"Sort of. I'm friends with her sister, who asked me to fill in. I'm afraid I'm not sure how to proceed."

She typed a series of commands into a laptop computer. After a moment she paused and looked back up at me. "According to my notes, Cammy's partner, Stone Silverman, has also left the completion."

"Yes. He was her fiancé and was obviously very distraught. I have a replacement for Stone who'll be here later this afternoon. I hope that's okay."

She nodded. "Given the circumstances, that will be fine. At the end of the day on Thursday, Team Honu was in second place. I'm afraid that after missing yesterday's competition and not receiving any points, it's now in ninth place out of ten teams, although we haven't yet entered the elimination round. That begins tomorrow, and the two teams with the lowest point total will be eliminated at the end of the day. Points are cumulative, so it's important for your team to score high enough to bring your total standing up to eighth place at a minimum if you want to continue."

I took a deep breath and let it out slowly. "Okay. Thank you for explaining that. How exactly does the whole thing work?"

She reached under the table and pulled out a briefcase. She opened it and took out a folder that contained several documents. Then she handed me what I assumed was an orientation packet. "Every morning at six a.m. local time, a clue will be emailed to each team. The email contains a link that provides a starting point for you to hack into the website specified and retrieve the information asked for. Keep in mind that this is a hack, not an easy entry, so I hope the brains part of your team is up to the challenge in this final round."

"I'm sure that won't be a problem." Based on what Luke had told me and I had observed, Zak could hack into anything given enough time, so I wasn't worried about that aspect of the contest at least. "Can any computer be used?"

"No. Each team has been provided with a computer that must be used throughout the competition. I'll have to find out what became of the computer assigned to Team Honu and have it brought to you as soon as possible."

"Does the hack occur in a centralized location or does each team handle it from their own room?"

"You're free to work from wherever you like as long as you use the assigned computer. Once the information is provided to the event coordinators, a clue will be revealed that will lead the team to a location on the island. If the clue is decoded correctly, and the team arrives at the destination intended, the team will be provided with a second clue that will lead to a second destination, followed by a third destination. Once the team reaches that final destination it looks for a phrase or set of numbers that must be entered in the computer. The first team to correctly post the message to the event site is awarded ten points for the day. The second team receives nine points and so on. Point totals are cumulative, so if a team receives ten points the first day and four the second, it would have a cumulative point total of seven. But, as I said, at the end of the day tomorrow the two teams with the lowest cumulative points will be eliminated. Do you have any questions at this point?"

"No." I glanced at the crowd that had gathered to meet the contestants. "I understand rooms are provided to the contestants."

"Yes." She typed several commands into the computer. "Team Honu was assigned to room 122. You can find it on the ground floor of the main wing."

It seemed to me the contest was a pretty sweet deal even for the teams that were eliminated early. All twenty contestants had been provided an all-expenses-paid stay at a luxury resort for the entire two weeks of the event, regardless of how long their team remained in the running for the money. "Zak and I aren't a couple, so we'll need a second room."

The woman frowned as she typed additional commands into the computer.

"I'm afraid all our standard rooms are booked. Hold on; I'll call over to the reception desk to see what we can do."

I waited while she spoke to someone on the phone. After a couple of minutes she hung up and returned her attention to me. "It looks like the resort has bungalows available, but I'm afraid the upgraded rooms will need to be paid for because they aren't included in the competition package."

I'd visited the huge lakeside mansion Zak and Zoe lived in and knew that paying for a beachfront bungalow wouldn't be an issue for a man who, Luke had indicated, had made a *lot* of money in the software industry, so I asked the woman to reserve one in Zak's name. Luke could stay with me in my room when he arrived on Monday, unless he too wanted to foot the bill for a bungalow. Even though Luke and I had been dating for almost a year, we'd never discussed finances, though based on what I'd observed, a beachfront bungalow wouldn't be an issue for him either should he decide he wanted an upgrade.

I did wonder about the lack of supervision as the contestants played the game. It didn't seem to me the event coordinators really cared whether the contestants had help. Given that the hacks could be accomplished from the privacy of your own room, I didn't see a way for the coordinators to monitor how many people were in a room when the hack was being accomplished.

It also seemed odd that, as a resident of the islands, they didn't have a problem with my acting as Cammy's substitute. It seemed they would realize I would have an advantage when it came to following the clues due to my familiarity with the area, although there could be locals competing and Maui was a popular vacation spot, so there could be others who'd spent time there. I supposed there wasn't an easy way to calculate how much time a contestant had spent here, so they hadn't made it an issue.

With all my questions answered and the team computer located, I headed to my room and called Luke. He'd only been gone for a week, but I really missed him. His trip hadn't been planned; his sister had suffered complications during the birth of her first child. We'd been on the mainland on vacation, so when he got the hysterical call from his mother he'd decided to go home for a few days before coming back to the islands. He'd invited me to go to Texas with him, but I hadn't wanted to meet his parents for the first time during such a stressful moment, so I'd flown home to Oahu while he made the side trip to Texas.

"How are you holding up?" Luke asked. I assumed he was referring to the fact that someone I knew had died, might very well have been murdered.

I sat down on a patio chair that had been provided on the lanai. It was a beautiful day and the view of the ocean from my room, while not quite that of a bungalow, was breathtaking. "I'm fine. I feel so bad for Bethany, but I didn't really know Cammy."

"You met Bethany on Oahu?"

"Yes. Bethany and I met at the Dolphin Bay Resort a few years ago. She grew up in Seattle but decided she wanted to move to the islands, so she got a job working in the surf shop at the resort. We met during an employee meeting and started to hang out from time to time. By the time she moved back to the mainland two years later we were good friends.

I felt my throat tighten as I glanced out over the lawn that separated the hotel from the white sand beach in the distance. The resort where the contestants were staying was in southwest Maui, which tended to be both hotter and drier than other parts of the island.

"And Bethany seems certain that her sister's accident wasn't just that? An accident?" Luke asked.

I put my bare feet up on the short wall in front of me as I willed myself to focus on the conversation rather than my confused emotions. "Bethany says Cammy never drank and there would have been absolutely no reason for her to start now. She also told me Cammy was concerned about something she'd discovered during the hacking part of the competition. Bethany is certain Cammy stumbled onto something she shouldn't have and was killed because of it."

"Like what?" Luke asked.

I sighed. "Bethany didn't know. I think it might be a good thing I was able to bring Zak on board. I'll need help from someone with the expertise not only to figure out the clues but to dig deeper to find whatever it was that had Cammy so freaked out."

"Are Zak and Zoe arriving today?"

"Yeah. They said they should be here by around six. Zak wants to get a feel for the computer that's been provided and maybe check around a bit with his own computer. I did find it sort of odd that at no point did the woman who explained the rules to me make any sort of statement about not having other people helping the teams. I think I'm going ask around about it just to be sure."

Luke paused and then said, "That does seem odd. You'd think every aspect of the contest would be monitored to prevent people from cheating."

"Can it be possible they don't care about that? Either things must be set up in such a way that cheating isn't an issue or they see it as part of the strategy. I guess once the event gets back underway tomorrow I'll get a better feel for things. Are you still planning on being here on Monday?"

"Yes. I would have come sooner, but my mom has some sort of a get-together planned for tomorrow. I'm flying directly into Kahului, so I should be at the resort by around one-thirty. You'll probably be out for the day, but we'll meet up as soon as you get back there. You can bring me up to speed and hopefully I can help the rest of the week."

"Do you have everything covered back at the ranch?"

Luke owned a horse ranch on Oahu. He'd hired temporary help to keep an eye on things while we were on vacation in Ashton Falls and he'd asked them to stay on while he was in Texas.

"Yeah. I have coverage for as long as I need it."

"Great. The more minds we throw at this the better. The awards ceremony is Sunday, which means we only have a week to figure out what's going on, and who, if anyone, is responsible for Cammy's death. I figure once everyone disperses it will be close to impossible to find the truth."

"Will the contestants who are eliminated leave immediately?" Luke asked.

"No. They want everyone here for the awards ceremony on Sunday, so everyone will continue to be put up at the resort for the entire week."

Luke didn't respond. I assumed he was thinking about everything I'd told him. I bet he found this contest as suspect as I did.

"So, how's your sister and your niece?" I asked after a brief pause of my own.

"Much better. My sister has been released from the hospital and the doctor thinks Kayla will be able to go home in a day or two. It was touch and go for a while, but I think everything will be fine."

"I'm so glad everything worked out. I'm sure it must have been terrifying for your family."

Luke let out a long sigh. "It was pretty bad. I saw my mom age ten years in front of my eyes when the doctor wasn't certain if either my sister or the baby were going to pull through. I'm afraid it would have killed her if things had turned out differently. And my poor brother-in-law. I can't imagine what must have been going through his mind."

I didn't say anything. I wasn't sure what there was to say. Luke's family had been through a terrifying experience.

I could hear someone speaking to him in the background. I knew he was staying with his parents, so he probably didn't have a lot of privacy.

"I gotta go," Luke said to me. "I'll try to call you back this evening."

"Okay. I love you."

Luke lowered his voice. "I love you too."

As I hung up, I tried to decide whether I should care that Luke obviously hadn't wanted whoever was in the room with him to hear him say he loved me. He might not have wanted to open that particular can of worms given the current circumstances, but I still felt somewhat wounded that he obviously hadn't informed his family that we were … I hesitated. We were what? I couldn't finish that sentence and it was only me talking quietly with myself in the privacy of my own head. Luke and I cared about each other, but due at least in part to my skittish feelings on the subject, we'd never discussed exactly what that meant.

I glanced at the waves breaking in the distance. I was a better person for having Luke in my life and he'd told me he loved me on many occasions, but I wondered if he thought of us in terms of permanence. There had been times when we'd joked about having a story to tell our grandkids, but did that mean Luke planned on us someday marrying and having children and grandchildren, or was that just the kind of thing people said without taking them seriously? I supposed I should be happy Luke hadn't brought up the subject of permanence and the commitment that came with it. Honestly, if Luke asked me to marry him, I had no idea what I'd say.

Oh, well. This was no time for introspection. Zak and Zoe would be here soon and I needed to get ready to bring them up to speed.

Chapter 2

Luke and I had met Zoe and Zak Zimmerman after I stumbled across a dead body floating in the lake while vacationing in their hometown of Ashton Falls and Zoe and I had worked together to find the killer. Like me, Zoe is petite yet extremely strong and athletic. She has blue eyes and long curly hair that seems to have a mind of its own yet totally works for her. She owns a wild and domestic animal rescue and rehabilitation shelter and is married to the computer software guru who'll be my teammate. Zoe and I met by chance, but we bonded almost immediately. It seemed we had a lot in common, including our propensity to becoming involved in everything even remotely interesting going on around us. Like Luke, Zak is a patient man. He seems willing to take a supporting role as she steamrolls through life.

When Zak and Zoe arrived at the resort and I explained the room situation, they decided to rent a two-bedroom oceanfront cottage that, conveniently, happened to be available. I hated to lodge on their dime even though I knew Zak was some sort of megamillionaire, but he pointed out that with all of us staying in the cottage, which provided two full suites plus a common kitchen and living area, it would be easier to plan our next moves and discuss strategy as the week progressed. Once we settled into the cottage, Zoe and I headed over to a restaurant to pick up some takeout for our dinner, while Zak familiarized himself with the computer we'd been assigned. Although they'd been to Maui before, they'd never visited this resort, so I took a few minutes to give Zoe the grand tour.

"There are three pools," I said as we walked through the center of the resort. "The one to the right is for adults only and is the best place to relax and maybe have a drink, if we even have time to relax. I'm not sure about that at this point. There's a lap pool near the gym that usually isn't crowded if you just want to get some exercise, and the largest pool to the left is a family pool that you'll probably want to avoid."

"Why?" Zoe asked after glancing toward it.

"Because of all the kids running and splashing."

Zoe smiled. "I like kids, but I get your point about the running and splashing. The grounds really are beautiful and the beach looks spectacular. I hope it works out that we have time to relax."

"You and Zak can always stay on after the contest is over," I suggested.

Zoe paused, looking around at the grounds surrounding us. "It would be tempting to extend the trip, but you remember, my best friend just had a baby. I hate to leave the kids with her for too long. And I decided not to bring Charlie on this trip, so I know he'll be missing me if I'm away for too long."

Zoe was referring to her dog, who usually went everywhere with her. I understood where she was coming from; I was missing my dog, Sandy, who was staying with my brother Jason and his family while I was away. My niece and nephew loved Sandy and he loved hanging out with him, but this trip, on the heels of the one to Ashton Falls, had left me feeling a deficiency in doggy cuddle time.

At the restaurant Zoe ordered a steak, a baked potato, a side salad, and a bottle of wine for Zak and a small salad and bottled water for herself. I ordered a sandwich with blackened Ono and a diet soda. We sat on a bench to the side of the hostess stand while we waited.

"I suppose we could just have ordered room service," I said.

"We could have," Zoe agreed, "but I enjoyed the walk. I'm feeling a little queasy after the long flight."

"Was it a bumpy ride?"

Zoe leaned back and placed a hand on her stomach. "Not really. I guess I just had a bad reaction. So, tell me what you know about the contest."

I filled Zoe in on everything I'd learned, which wasn't much.

Zoe paid close attention as I spoke. "You said there are ten teams in the final round. Do you know anything about the other nine?" Zoe asked.

"Not really. I did overhear a couple of the contestants talking about the team in first place. They're a brother and sister from Canada. I'm not sure how they're able to find the clues that much faster than anyone else, but based on what I heard, they've pretty much been in first place during the entire contest, including the preliminary rounds, which were held in different locations around the country."

Zoe narrowed her gaze as she appeared to be considering the situation. "So the entire contest hasn't been held in Hawaii?"

"No. Just this final round. Bethany said this is the fourth location. There were originally a hundred teams and just the highest-ranking ten came to Maui." I paused as I tried to remember what else Bethany had told me. "I think the other rounds were in Boston, Chicago, and San Francisco."

Zoe tilted her head. "So it doesn't seem that any one team would necessarily have a home field advantage."

I shook my head. "No, it doesn't seem like it. I guess if one team has been in the lead the entire time they must have an advantage at the computer."

Zoe pulled her legs up onto the bench, tucking them under her. "If that's the case I have a feeling they aren't going to be thrilled to find out that Zak is here."

I smiled. "Yeah, I guess not. Although I don't care about winning. I'm here to find out what happened to Cammy, not collect the million-dollar grand prize."

"I agree," Zoe said. "We'll just play well enough to stay in the game, but we won't play to win. In fact, if we play too well we might gain attention we don't want. It'll be easier to snoop around if we aren't seen as a threat. We might want to aim to maintain a position somewhere in the middle of the pack. I bet it's going to get pretty cutthroat at the top."

I shrugged. "Yeah, I guess."

Zoe and I headed back to the cottage when our order was ready. I had to hand it to Zak; he'd set up an entire command center during the time we were gone. Not only was the computer I'd been given to use in the contest up and running but he had two laptops of his own set up as well.

"Aren't you afraid someone is going to mess with your equipment while we're away from the cottage?" I asked. The computers he'd brought probably cost more than the truck Luke had purchased recently.

"I plan to take the laptops with us when we leave. And I left instructions at the desk that we weren't to be disturbed and wouldn't require maid service. We can trade out the towels and linens as necessary. I thought it might be best not to have people snooping around while we're out."

"I got you a steak," Zoe informed him. "Take a break and eat it before it gets cold."

Zak turned in his chair and looked at his wife. "You only got a salad?"

"I'm not really hungry," Zoe answered.

I could see the tenderness in Zak's eyes turn to concern. "You still aren't feeling well?"

Zoe took a bite of her salad, then swallowed and smiled in his direction. "I'm fine. Just tired, I guess. Did you get a look at the computer the contest provided?"

Zak, who was tall and fit, with blond hair and blue eyes, sat down next to Zoe. He kissed her cheek before he took the lid off his takeout container and began to add toppings to his potato. "I did. The memory has been erased, but I can recover what was there with the software on my personal laptop. I'm not sure the computer ever held any important information, but if Lani's friend really did stumble onto something while performing one of the hacks required for the contest, and if that's what got her killed, I'm going to assume it was while using this computer." Zak turned and looked at me. "Are you certain this is the same computer she used?"

I shook my head. "No, not really. That's what I was told, but I don't know it for a fact."

"Do you know if Cammy told her partner what she found?" Zak asked me.

I paused. "Maybe. I can call Bethany to ask her for Stone's contact information. It seems logical Cammy would share what she found with him, although from what I understand, he was the brawn part of the team, so he might not have understood what she told him. Still, it couldn't hurt to ask. I'll call Bethany as soon as I finish eating."

"While you have Bethany on the phone, ask her if Cammy mentioned anything else about the contest," Zoe suggested. "She might have offered little tidbits about the other contestants or the direction she felt the competition was headed. It occurred to me that if Cammy was pushed and it wasn't by someone trying to hide whatever she discovered, it could have been by one of her competitors."

I frowned. "You think one of the other contestants might have pushed her?"

"Her team was in second place. Maybe the first-place team was feeling threatened or the third-place team wanted to eliminate the barrier right ahead of them."

"But to kill someone over a contest?"

Zoe shrugged. "Unfortunately, I've seen people kill for a lot less than the million-dollar prize. Do you know where the accident occurred?"

I nodded. "It's not far from here. Just down the beach."

"Maybe after we eat we can take a walk down there to look at things. I'm not sure there will be anything to find, but it seems like a prudent thing to do."

After dinner Zak went back to the computers and Zoe and I walked down the beach to the bluff where I knew Cammy had fallen. It was a warm evening with a slight, cooling breeze, so there were a lot of resort guests out and about, taking a stroll or watching the sunset.

"I think the sunsets are one of my favorite memories from my first trip to Maui," Zoe said. "It was so lovely walking on the beach with Zak, hand in hand, as the sun dipped into the sea."

"They do seem to be a visitor favorite. So you've just been here the one time?"

Zoe nodded. "Zak and I have talked about coming for another trip, but so far we haven't made it back. I really would like to come for a romantic getaway if we can work out the scheduling. Maybe for our anniversary. Zak proposed to me on the beach on that trip."

I smiled. "You got engaged on Maui?"

Zoe shook her head. "No. Zak proposed on Maui, but I'm afraid I didn't answer him until Halloween, which would be when the official engagement took place."

I stopped walking. "Didn't you tell me that you were on Maui in June?"

Zoe nodded.

"And you didn't accept Zak's proposal until October?"

Zoe smiled. "I know to look at us now we seem like an old married couple without a doubt in the world, but I was a huge mess for a very long time. I had all sorts of commitment issues that I couldn't seem to get past, despite the fact that I loved Zak and wanted to spend the rest of my life with him. When he proposed I panicked. Of course Zak knows me better than I know myself at times. He knew I would freak out when he popped the question, so after he asked me to marry him, he told me not to answer him until I had a chance to think things over. Looking back, I have no idea why it took me four months to realize Zak was the love of my life and that I wanted to be with him always. There were times I wanted to run away, but looking at my life from my current perspective, I realize what a huge mistake that would have been." Zoe paused and looked at me. "I've learned something important during the past several years and that's to follow my heart. That may seem trite, but when I remember that I almost talked myself out of a life with Zak it makes me realized how very illogical the mind can be."

I couldn't help but grin. I'm not sure why I felt such a huge rush of relief, but I did. Maybe I figured if Zoe, who was obviously in a deeply happy, committed relationship, could have been so insecure as to keep her future husband waiting for four months for an answer to his marriage proposal, there was hope for me. I wanted to thank Zoe for sharing what she had, but I wasn't sure what to say, so I continued to the cliff from which Cammy had fallen.

When we arrived at the spot where I'd been told the tragedy had occurred we paused. We both looked over the side. The drop was substantial, but not so precipitous as to indicate that a fall would absolutely result in death. There were large rocks at the bottom of the cliff, but there were also sandy patches. I thought it was possible if you fell in the right spot from the right angle you could end up with no more than a broken bone or two as a result. Zoe had suggested that perhaps one of the other contestants had pushed Cammy. Could that person have been trying to injure rather than kill her? Somehow I doubted that would end up being the case, but if it was a reasonable enough explanation it should be explored.

******

Back at the cottage, Zoe said she was exhausted and headed off to bed. I called Bethany while Zak shut down the computers and headed to the bedroom behind her. It wasn't all that late, but with the time change I could see why Zak and Zoe were both tired. I had a feeling tomorrow was going to be a long and challenging day, so I poured myself a glass of the wine Zoe had brought for Zak but he hadn't drunk, then went out onto the lanai to relax as the sky darkened.

I realized that with the time difference there was a good chance Bethany would have already gone to bed, so instead of calling her, I texted, asking her to call me when she had the opportunity. My phone rang a few minutes later.

"Did you find out anything?" Bethany asked immediately.

I leaned back in my lounge chair. "No, not really. Zak and Zoe Zimmerman are here and I think they're going to be a lot of help. They were wondering if you'd had a chance to speak to Stone. Zoe thought maybe Cammy had talked to him about what she'd found that concerned her."

Bethany sighed. "No. I haven't talked to Stone about anything. He's so broken up about Cammy's death that I haven't wanted to make it worse by grilling him."

"Do you think Cammy would have discussed her concerns with him?" I asked.

Bethany was quiet for a moment and then said, "Yes, I think she would have. Stone isn't techy like Cammy, so I don't know that she would have gone into a lot of detail, but if she found something disturbing I think she would have shared her concerns with him. I'll try to talk to him tomorrow. I know he's really hurting, but I imagine that if he feels there's a way to help find the monster who did this to Cammy, he'll want to help."

I hesitated before I continued. I knew I needed to tread lightly so I wouldn't further upset Bethany. "Zoe and I took a walk to the cliff where..." I let my thought trail off. "It's high, but not that high, and there are rocks but also beach. Do you think it's possible Cammy was pushed because she and Stone were in second place in the competition rather than because of some computer conspiracy?"

"You think one of the contestants killed her to better their own chances?"

"I don't know. Maybe someone pushed her to injure her, but she fell wrong. I'm not saying that's what happened, but if you're going to speak to Stone maybe you can ask him about the other competitors. It would be good for us to get a feel for who exactly we're up against. He was competing against the entire field for the whole competition and we're just starting. Any tips he might have could come in handy."

"Okay," Bethany agreed. "I'll talk to him. I'm not sure if he'll be able to share what he knows, but I'll try."

"Call me either way."

"All right. And Lani—be careful. I'm so very grateful you agreed to look into things, but I don't want you getting hurt. If Cammy did die because one of the competitors wanted her out of the way I'm afraid you might pose the same threat."

"I'll be careful and I won't get hurt," I said, hoping deep inside that I would be able to keep that promise.

Chapter 3

Sunday, April 30

When I entered the common area of the cottage the next morning Zak was already up. His hair was wet, so I assumed he'd showered before dressing in blue denim shorts and a white T-shirt. I offered a greeting, but he didn't reply. He seemed to be focused intently on whatever he was doing on the computer, which I figured was a good thing, so I headed into the kitchen and poured myself a cup of coffee. It was early, only a little after five, so the sky was still dark, but I knew the first hint of dawn would appear at any moment. I stepped out onto the lanai and sipped my coffee as I watched the moon set behind the island in the distance. It was already warm, which meant a hot day even though the long days of summer had yet to arrive.

I had lived in Hawaii my entire life, so I was used to the heat and humidity, but I worried about my friends from a mountain climate should the barometer climb too high. I made a mental note to remind them to use plenty of sunscreen and pack lots of water. It never ceased to amaze me the number of tourists who arrived for a two-week stay after months of planning but without bothering to take precautions with hats and sunscreen. Too often, after a single day on the beach said tourists would spend the remainder of their vacation in their rooms getting over nasty sunburns.

I sat down on a lounge chair and glanced at my phone. I saw I had a text from Luke, wishing me good morning and good luck. I knew it was five hours later in Texas, which meant it was already midmorning for him. He'd said his mother had a party planned for that afternoon, but I hoped he'd be available for a quick chat that morning, so I texted him and waited for a reply.

He didn't answer after a couple of minutes, so I headed inside to take my own shower and dress in preparation for the day ahead. The email that would provide the starting point for the day's events was due to come through at six a.m., so I figured I had plenty of time to get ready, maybe even grab a bite to eat before we got started.

When I returned to the common area I found Zoe curled up on the sofa with a bottle of water and Zak still busy at the computer. I poured myself a second cup of coffee and sat down across from Zoe, who was dressed in khaki-colored shorts and a sunny yellow top.

"Are you feeling better this morning?" I asked her.

"Much." Zoe's eyes sparkled. "I guess I just needed a good night's sleep. I really, really hate the reason we're participating in this event, but I do find I have a certain amount of enthusiasm now that the contest is upon us."

"I have to say I agree," I admitted. "It's going to be hard to maintain our prospective and not get caught up in the competition. I wasn't following the race before this, but Bethany did tell me the clues are in the form of puzzles or riddles to solve, and I've always loved a good puzzle."

"I've been thinking about the clues," Zoe said. "If the same person or group of people are creating them I'm guessing there's some sort of pattern. After four weeks the teams will have figured that out. I'm afraid we're going to be at a huge disadvantage."

I shrugged. "Maybe. But we have Zak, and I'm willing to bet he's a more proficient hacker than anyone else, and we have me, who spends a fair amount of time on Maui thanks to having a brother living here. I'm also pretty good with local culture and history, and I know the language." I paused. "Well, to a degree. All we really need to do the first few days is stay in the running. I'm hoping by the end of the week, when the competition becomes fiercer, we'll have settled into a rhythm."

Zoe tilted her head. "I'm sure you're right. I don't know what I can bring to the table, but I'm happy to help however I can."

I got up from the sofa and went back into the kitchen. I topped off Zak's coffee and refilled my own. There wasn't a lot I was going to be able to do to help until after Zak completed the hacking part of the challenge, so I settled back on the sofa to check my emails and text messages. There was one from my mother, reminding me that I'd promised to come for dinner that evening. Dang. I'd forgotten all about that. She knew Luke was in Texas, so she'd taken advantage of the fact that I wouldn't be spending the day with him to invite me to spend the evening with her, my father, and the young boy they were fostering. I should call to explain what was going on, but I knew she'd read me the riot act for putting myself in the middle of yet another murder investigation, so I texted her instead, explaining that something had come up and I was on Maui for a few days and would need to reschedule dinner.

There was also a text from my cousin and best friend, Kekoa, asking how things were going so far. I texted back with the condensed version of the situation. Luke still hadn't answered my text from earlier, which had me frowning. It seemed that even if he was busy with his family he could find the time to type out a few words in reply. Of course it was possible he was somewhere that didn't have cell service.

"Okay, we have the email," Zak announced from the table where the three computers were set up. "It seems pretty straightforward. Just give me a minute."

I was expecting a minute to turn into an hour—Bethany had said the hacks had become more complicated as the contest progressed—but Zak was in and had retrieved the required information in an actual minute.

"That was fast," I said admiringly.

Zak was frowning. "It was an easy hack. Too easy. I have a feeling it was a test of some sort. Given the fact that we're new to the contest, it could be that the event organizers are taking it easy on us the first day."

"Do you think they know how quickly you got in?" I asked.

"They know. Someone is monitoring every keystroke, which is why I'll be using my own computer to conduct the snooping-around portion of the day."

"So do we have the first clue?" Zoe asked from her position on the sofa.

"Hang on," Zak instructed. I imagined he was delivering the information the contest organizers asked for, as instructed. After a minute or so the contest computer dinged, alerting us that we had a new email, which contained only four words.

"'Where the queen played,'" Zak read aloud. He sat back in his chair while Zoe turned to look at me.

"Queen?" she asked.

"Hawaii was once a kingdom, so there are quite a few references to royalty on the islands," I explained. "The Queen Ka'ahumanu Center is a shopping complex in Kahului. The clue could be leading to that, although it seems to refer to the past, while the shopping center is very modern. There's a church in Wailuku named after Queen Ka'ahumanu. The current structure was built in the late 1800s, but there's been a church of some sort on that site since ancient times. It's only open on Sundays, so that could be it, though the clue says where the queen *played*, not where she *prayed*."

I paused and tried to think of other options. "There's a sacred area currently known as Maluuluolele Park, built over a royal residence called Moku'ula. I suppose a queen could have played there. It might not be a bad place to look for a clue." I took a breath, narrowed my eyes, and pursed my lips. "The town of Lahaina was once the home of royalty on Maui, so, again, I suppose it's possible there are many locations there where a queen could have played."

Zak was typing on the computer as I considered the possibilities. Zoe was simply watching quietly from her spot on the sofa. She seemed interested in what was going on, yet content to take on a passive role.

"What about the Queen Theatre?" Zak asked, turning from the computer to look at me. "According to this website, the theater is gone, but the building, which is in Lahaina, still stands."

I smiled. "That does fit the clue the best of anything I've suggested so far. It seems all roads lead to Lahaina, or at least that part of the island, so I think we should head in that direction. We'll check out the old theater and if we don't find the second clue we'll try one of the other options."

Zak offered to drive, so I took the backseat, offering Zoe the passenger seat up front. The drive took about thirty minutes, which gave Zoe and me the opportunity to chat about the scenery while we traveled. It was a clear and sunny day with nary a cloud in sight. Like Zoe, I was very much saddened by the reason behind our participation in the event but undeniably enjoying the adrenaline created by the chase now that it was underway. The fact that the Queen Theatre was in Lahaina would be easily discovered by anyone who thought to cross-reference *queen* with Maui, so I assumed the second clue, if we were correct about the first one, would be harder to figure out. If the clues weren't

46

going to be a bit more challenging I had to wonder why the prize was a very generous million dollars.

In Lahaina, Zak parked in one of the hourly lots down a narrow side street. It was early in the day, so the cute though touristy town wasn't yet crowded, as I knew it would be later in the morning. The old theater currently housed an art gallery and a T-shirt shop, neither of which were open yet. It was only a little after seven, and I knew the shops wouldn't be open for another two or even three hours.

"Now what?" Zoe asked. "Do we just wait around for the shops to open?"

"No," I decided. "The event organizers knew it would only take us a little while to crack an encryption this easy and then figure out that the Queen Theatre was most likely the answer to the first clue. They would know we'd get here before the shops opened."

We all looked around, trying to work out what we should do next.

"You know what's strange?" Zak said after a moment. "We seem to be the only ones here. If there are ten teams and they all have the same clues doesn't it seem as if at least some of the others should have figured it out by now?"

Zak had a point. The hack had been easy. The first clue was easy. So far everything was just a little bit too easy for my taste.

"The theater might be the obvious answer; maybe it isn't the right answer," Zoe voiced the conclusion we'd all come to.

I paused before I jumped on the wrong-clue train. Maybe the fact that the theater was too easy and therefore should be discounted was part of the strategy. Before we simply left in favor of one of the other options I felt it was prudent to think things through a bit. "Unless," I countered, "it's the correct location and we don't need to go inside to get the next clue." I stood looking at the building from across the street. There was a sign out front that said, "Queen Theatre Building 1933." That could be a clue or a code of some sort. There was also a poster in a glass case between the art studio and the T-shirt shop. The case was the kind that opened so whatever was inside could be changed. Today there was a print of a painting depicting a baby swaddled in white cloth, sleeping in what appeared to be a cave. Beneath the photo were the words *aina hanau*. I knew that meant birthplace in Hawaiian.

"Hāna," I said.

"Hāna?" Zoe asked.

"The painting of the baby in the cave. Ka'ahumanu was the favorite wife of the first King Kamehameha and acted as regent of the Kingdom of Hawaii. It's said she was born in a cave near Hāna, on the southeast end of Maui. The cave can be reached via a moderate hike."

"And the drive to get to the trailhead?" Zoe asked.

"It isn't more than seventy-five miles by car, but the road is narrow and winding. It'll take about two and a half hours at this time of day if we drive straight through."

We all stood staring at one another. If we were wrong and our real destination wasn't the birthplace of Ka'ahumanu, we'd be wasting a huge chunk of the day. The woman I'd spoken to the previous day had told me Team Honu was currently in ninth place and that two teams would be cut by the end of the day. To come out in eighth place or better, we probably needed to finish in the top six or seven, although it was difficult to calculate more exactly without knowing the actual point totals of each team.

It was still bothering me that we seemed to be the only team at the theater. Zak had cracked the code, allowing him to hack into the site pretty darn fast, which meant we most likely hadn't been the last team to arrive at the theater, but even if we'd been the first team here at least one other team should have shown up by now. I looked up and down the street at the small shops, most of which weren't open yet. There were a few people wandering around, but not so many that it should have been difficult to pick out others who would have been overly interested in the same building we were. Zak had expressed surprise that he'd hacked into the internet location indicated so easily. Could he have missed a step? Was there something else to find?

"What now?" Zoe eventually asked, after none of us had spoken for several minutes.

I glanced at Zak, who was waiting for me to lead the way.

"How certain are you that you hacked into the correct site and there wasn't anything else to find?" I asked Zak.

"Absolutely certain. The hack was easy, which, as I said, I found odd, given the fact that we're in the finals, but I went where it took me and there was nothing else other than the four words I shared."

"Do you think someone—maybe one of the other competitors—hacked into the system and fed us false information?" Zoe asked.

"I suppose it's possible," Zak admitted. "The system used for the contest is closed but only moderately protected. If I wanted to, I could hack in and alter the information provided to the others. And if I could there are others who can as well."

I took a deep breath and let it out slowly. I knew I needed to make up my mind, and quickly. Even if the birthplace of Ka'ahumanu was the correct clue, we had no way of knowing whether there was an additional clue or it was the last destination for the day. If there was a third clue time would be of the essence.

"Okay," I decided. "The hike to the cave is a fairly easy one, so I think Zoe and I should head in that direction. Zak, we'll drop you back at the resort. Take another look around to see if you can figure out whether the others received the same information. If you find anything strange call or text Zoe."

Zak glanced at Zoe, who nodded. "I think that's a good plan," she said. "If Zak finds something we missed we can react accordingly."

I looked around the area one last time before we went back to the car. It continued to bother me that no one else was around. Bethany was counting on me to figure out what had happened to Cammy, and that would be a lot more difficult if Team Honu was eliminated from the contest on the first day. Maybe I should have asked more questions when I had the chance. If we were missing a step it was going to be too late to change direction and adjust our course by the time we figured it out.

Chapter 4

Hāna was a beautiful area littered with tall waterfalls and lush greenery. If we were simply doing the tourist thing I'd be driving slowly and stopping frequently along the way to enjoy the scenery that had to be experienced up close and personal to be truly appreciated.

The road was something of a loop that meandered along the shore toward the very southern tip of the island and then through the high country on the way back to the west. Most tourists drove the loop clockwise, often creating tremendous traffic jams as they stopped to appreciate the sites along the way, so I'd decided to do the opposite, approaching Hāna through the high country rather than along the eastern shore.

"Tell me about the area," Zoe said as she hung her head out of the window, enjoying the coolness of the spring morning.

"The high country is a series of small towns occupied with locals, many of whom farm the land. Haleakalā, the dormant volcano that climbs to ten thousand feet, is to your left. It's an awesome experience to drive to the top and then hike down into the crater, but we'll have to leave that for another day."

Zoe took in a deep breath and let it out slowly. "It really is spectacular and much cooler than the coast."

"It can be downright frigid at the top of the volcano, which can offer a nice change on a hot summer day."

Zoe and I traveled in silence for a while as I focused on the road and she took in the scenery. Eventually she brought up Cammy's murder again, asking if I had seen the police report.

"Not yet," I admitted. "My brother John is a detective for Maui PD. He's a levelheaded guy, not prone to overreacting, but he's the oldest of us and can sometimes be overprotective. I'm not sure how he'll respond to me intentionally snooping around in the case. I have another brother, Jeff, who works for MPD. He's the closest to me in age and by far the least protective. I'm not sure he'd have access to as much information as John, but it wouldn't hurt to contact him to see what he knows."

"And you said your brother who works for the Honolulu PD is named Jason. Three Js in one family seems like a lot."

"Actually, there are five," I corrected her. "John, Jason, Jimmy, Justin, and Jeff, or the J team, as my mom refers to them."

"I guess that's kind of fun. Confusing but fun. So why aren't you named Jane or something else beginning with a J?"

"My grandmother insisted that I have a traditional Hawaiian name and there aren't any beginning with J. Personally, I'm just as happy to have my own identity. It can be difficult to make your own way when you're always seen as some sort of an extension of your brothers."

Zoe turned and looked at me. "I can see your point, but you're also very lucky. I can't tell you how much I longed for a sibling when I was growing up. At least I had my best friends, Levi and Ellie, who were like siblings in a way. Still, it isn't the same."

I smiled. "No, I guess not. And I do love my brothers. It annoys me that they still treat me like a kid, but I know any one of them would take a bullet for me."

"So call John. Ask him what he knows. Zak could probably hack in and get it, but he won't want to. It'll be better if John tells us what we need to know."

I nodded. "Okay. I'll call him later. For now, let's focus on the birthplace. Hopefully we'll find the clue we need and all these doubts stomping through my head will be put to rest."

"It does feel off that everything is coming to us so easily," Zoe agreed. "It's almost like they provided a diversion and we fell for it."

"We're close to our destination," I told her. "I guess all we can do is stay the course and then reassess the situation when we get to the cave."

"We've come too far to turn back now."

I found a place to park near the pier at Hāna Bay and we headed up the trail. There were places that had been washed out over time, but for two women in their twenties, both of whom were in exceptionally good shape, it was almost as easy as a walk in the park. When we arrived at the site of the cave we found a plaque depicting the name of the person being honored and the dates she lived. Nothing exceptional, nothing that in any way resembled a clue to a third location or a code that could be entered in the computer after completing the activities for the day.

There were, however, four other people on the trail I recognized from the resort the previous day. Two were coming down the trail as we climbed up and two were coming up behind us as we stood looking at the plaque wondering what to do.

Think, Lani, think!

The fact that I had seen people from the resort here made me feel better after not seeing anyone familiar at the theater earlier. Zak had texted Zoe while we were on the way to let her know the clues the others had received had been the same, but their hacks had been quite a bit more difficult, so it had taken them longer to get through to the four words we'd found so easily. While the initial clues had been the same, all the hacks were different.

"The team heading down the mountain obviously got here ahead of us despite the fact that they got a later start," I commented. "I don't know how many others are ahead of us, but at least one is behind." I nodded toward the pair still making their way up the trail. "We need to find the next clue and get a move on."

Zoe walked around to the cave entrance behind the plaque. She peered at the rocky surface, then ran her hand slowly over it. "There's something carved into the rock."

I left my spot near the plaque and joined her. There was a single word: *green*.

I frowned. Green? Did it refer to the color green? I was totally at a loss. There was a chance someone with the last name Green could have written the word on the rock and it had nothing to do with the contest, but I didn't see anything else that looked like it could be a clue.

"Do you have reception on your phone?" I asked Zoe.

She pulled her phone out of her pocket and looked at it. "No, I'm afraid not."

I hesitated, wondering what to do. Green could be a code or cypher. If we could get hold of Zak we could ask his opinion.

"Let's head back to the car," I said with a feeling of dread in my stomach. "We'll call Zak to see what he makes of this."

"Okay." Zoe squeezed my hand in a show of support.

The team who had been coming up the hill behind us stood at the plaque, staring at it. Part of me wanted to wait to see what they'd do, but time of the essence and I had no idea whether they'd have any better luck than we'd had. For all

I knew, all the other teams were ahead of us. It occurred to me that there didn't seem to be any rules as to how the clue sites could be accessed, and there was a small airport in Hāna. Could the other teams in the lead have chartered a small plane, allowing them to arrive here long before us? If we made it through this first round I'd need to think like a competitor, not like a friend desperately trying to help someone close to her find closure in the midst of tragedy.

Back at the car, Zoe called Zak to tell him about the word. He chatted with her while he ran it through several programs, but, judging by her responses, he wasn't finding anything in terms of a code or cypher. I decided to head into town in search of food while he checked. We'd never eaten that morning and I was starving.

There were very few places to eat, but I chose the Barefoot Café, which was essentially a burger shack. I asked Zoe what she wanted, then went to order while she continued to speak with Zak. While I waited for our food I sat down on a bench. I checked my phone only to see there still was no text from Luke. I knew he was busy and I shouldn't be bothered that he hadn't had time to get back to me, but as

I looked out over the bay all I could feel was a sad emptiness. Most of that probably came from my sorrow over what had happened to Cammy, but at least part of it was that I was getting used to Luke being part of my everyday life and I missed him terribly when he wasn't with me. I wasn't sure if that was a good thing or a bad one.

"Order for Lani," a man called out. I got up and went to collect the burgers and sodas I'd ordered.

"Anything?" I asked Zoe, who was giggling at something Zak had said as I returned to the car.

"Yup. Zak found out that the man who was the pastor at the Ka'ahumanu Church in Wailuku when the queen was alive was Johnathan Smith Green."

Wow. I had to hand it to Zak. He'd really come through. "That husband of yours really is a genius," I said to Zoe.

"Yeah." She smiled. "He really is."

"Let's eat and then get back on the road. It'll take us at least three hours to get to Wailuku. Hopefully that will be the last stop for the day."

******

The church at Wailuku was white-steepled, built on a site that had previously held services in nothing more than a simple shed. Ka'ahumanu was an early Hawaiian convert to Christianity, and it was her influence that led to the arrival of missionaries on the islands. The present building was two stories tall with a bell tower that featured a clock. Services were held every Sunday, with hymns and invocation in Hawaiian. The front door was locked when we arrived, so I hoped the words or numbers we needed to enter in the computer would be easily accessible from the exterior.

Zoe and I circled the building, looking for something, although we had no idea what that might be. I wondered if the church had been unlocked earlier and we'd gotten there too late. After I felt we'd examined the building as carefully as we possibly could I found myself standing in front of it and just staring at it, as if willing it to speak, to give me the answer I needed.

"Do you see anything at all?" I asked Zoe.

She looked around the building and the surroundings again. "It does seem as if the clue would be hidden inside. I wonder if there's a way to get in that won't damage anything."

I took a deep breath and tried to focus. There were windows around the side of the building, all of which appeared to be closed. The roof was pitched, and although there was a second story, there was only one window at the front. The tower was tall and impressive, with several levels. There were windows—one in the front and several on the side, just above the roofline—in the first, followed by the clock, then the bell, and last a narrow steeple. It seemed getting in through one of those windows would be my best bet. The problem was, I'd need to get up to the roof first. I looked around for a place to start my climb and finally settled on a nearby tree. I'd need to take a leap of faith from the closest branch to the sloped roof, but I did a few calculations and, with enough force, I thought I could make it. Luckily, there were shrubs below to break my fall if I was wrong.

I explained my plan to Zoe and then scrambled up the tree I'd picked out. There was a gap between the tree and the roof, so I climbed just a bit higher than I thought I needed to so that I'd be able to both leap and land in the right location.

"Be careful," Zoe called from below as I identified the best place to launch my body and settled into place.

"Don't worry. I've got this," I called back.

Once I was set as best I could, I scrunched down and leaped toward the roof. I let out a long breath when my feet landed safely. I leaned forward so as not to lose my footing and slip down the steep angle of the roof. I caught my breath, then started up the roof toward the tower. As I'd hoped, the window wasn't locked. I carefully climbed through and then headed down the stairs. The tall windows along the side of the building provided plenty of light. There were wooden pews and an altar arranged in front of a cross on the far wall, a warm and welcoming place for weekly worship. I'd never attended services here, but now that I could see how charming it was I found I very much wanted to.

Once I got my bearings I began to look around, though I had no idea exactly what I was looking for or how well it would be hidden. I was looking under and around each pew when I heard banging on one of the windows. I looked up and saw Zoe outside, waving her arms.

"I haven't found it yet," I called to her.

"The team that was behind us at the cave arrived a minute ago. They went to the big tree in the front, wrote something down, and left. I checked it out and there are numbers carved in the trunk. I think those are the numbers we need."

Great. I'd just done the Spider-Man thing for nothing. I should have known the event coordinators wouldn't want ten teams breaking into a church. Of course carving into the trunk of a monkey pod tree wasn't exactly environmentally friendly.

"Okay. I'll get out the way I climbed in. Find something in the car to write down the numbers."

Zoe held up her phone. "I have them. I already sent them to Zak."

"Perfect. Just give me a minute."

I went back up the stairs, out the window, down the side of the roof, and leaped toward the closest tree branch, which, fortunately, I was able to hang on to. Then I scrambled down the tree and returned to Zoe.

"Zak entered the numbers as soon as I sent them to him. He called and told me they were correct and we were the seventh team to check in."

I blew out a breath. "Good. I'm glad the assumptions we made turned out okay. Let's go back to the resort and relax for a bit. If we make the cut tomorrow we'll most likely be just as exhausted."

Chapter 5

We decided to eat dinner in so we could use the time to come up with a strategy for the following day. Zak had spent a good part of the day doing some cybersnooping and I was curious to find out what he'd come up with. Zoe and I both headed in to take showers while Zak ordered the food.

I closed my eyes as the cool water ran over my head and down my body. The tension in my neck was beginning to give me a headache. When Bethany had called to explain the situation I hadn't taken time to think things through; I'd simply reacted, agreeing to fill in for Cammy to find her killer. Now that I had time to reflect, I was beginning to experience doubts about how and why the whole thing had occurred in the first place.

I poured shampoo into my hand, then worked it into my hair. Just a week ago Luke and I had been in Ashton Falls, enjoying some alone time on the lakeshore. Then his sister had gone into labor and he'd left for Texas, requiring me to travel home on my own. I'd barely had a chance to unpack when Bethany had called and I was heading off to save the day. If I were honest with myself, I was emotionally and physically drained, yet I knew helping my friend was the right thing to do.

After I rinsed my hair and dried off I dressed in a clean pair of shorts and a T-shirt and headed into the common area to find the food had arrived. I grabbed my dinner and sat down next to Zoe. She was nibbling on a salad with garlic bread while I began packing into a huge hamburger and Zak took a forkful of grilled fish and rice. It was a beautiful evening, and we decided to take the rest of our meal out onto the lanai, where we could watch the sun set. Luke still hadn't called or texted, so I sent him another text in case he hadn't received the first one.

"Does anyone think it's strange that there were ten teams and we only saw a couple of them the entire day?" I asked after I'd eaten several bites of my burger.

"While the clues, once the teams hit the road, seem to be the same for everyone, the hacks are individual," Zak responded. "Some are much harder than others. We completed our hack first. By a lot, which is why we didn't see anyone else at the theater. The next team took thirty additional minutes and the last one to complete their hack took almost three hours. Because the first clue isn't provided until the hack has been complete the field is strung out."

"Having such a huge degree of difficulty between the hacks doesn't seem fair when the points given at the end of the day is first come, most points," Zoe pointed out.

"Yes, and with only one day's data at my fingertips I can't tell if the hacks are assigned randomly or if there's a method to determining who gets the easiest and who gets the hardest hack. I do think our supereasy hack was intentional for today. I'm guessing it was a test to see if we were worthy of being in the finals. If we hadn't accomplished the hack in short order it's my opinion we would have been eliminated with an intentionally impossible hack tomorrow."

"Coming in seventh given the fact that we solved the hack way ahead of anyone else is pretty bad," I concluded. "We need a better strategy if we make it through this round."

"We did make it," Zak confirmed. "I got a text while you were both in the shower. We're currently in eighth place based on cumulative points. Eight teams will compete tomorrow and two more teams will be eliminated at the end of the day. That will leave six teams going into Tuesday's competition. According to the schedule, one team will be eliminated on Tuesday and then one each on Wednesday, Thursday, and Friday. That will leave the top two in the finals on Saturday."

I dipped one of my fries in ketchup as I let everything noodle around in my brain for a bit. I had no way of knowing how hard tomorrow's hack would be, but one thing was certain: if we were going to stay in the race beyond tomorrow I was right about needing a better strategy. Luke was due to be here tomorrow afternoon, which meant we'd have his help on Tuesday unless someone informed us that extra help was frowned upon between now and then.

The race aside, I had to stay mindful of the fact that what we were really trying to do was figure out what had happened to Cammy. I should call John, although part of me feared if he found out why I was on Maui he'd come up with a way to put a stop to my involvement in the case.

"Did you find out anything about the other teams?" I asked Zak.

He nodded. "Kimmy and Kenny Carter are the brother-and-sister team from Canada who've been in first place leading up to this week. As far as I know, they still are after today."

"There was a Kimmy and a Cammy in the same contest?" Zoe asked, surprise apparent in her voice.

"Seems so," Zak answered. "I discovered something curious about the Carter team."

"Which is?" Lani asked.

"For one thing, neither Kimmy nor Kenny seems to have a background in computers. I can't find where either has a technology-related degree or worked in a computer-related industry. And their hack was the easiest second only to ours, yet they took a full forty minutes to work through it."

"That is interesting," I commented.

Zak held up his hand. "That's not the interesting part. "I was able to hack into the monitoring software used by the contest organizers. Kimmy and Kenny were on the totally wrong track with their hack and then, suddenly, they were in."

"You think someone helped them," I concluded.

"I know someone did. That piqued my curiosity, so I did some more digging. Kimmy has one of those fitness watches that records not only your steps but the route you took. I hacked into her account—by the way, her password is Kimmy C—and found out she at least didn't go to Lahaina. It's possible Kenny went alone, but I'm guessing the clue they received led them directly to Hāna."

I took a minute to let that sink in. It seemed as if the event coordinators were helping Kimmy and Kenny, but why? If anyone else caught on to what they were doing there would be hell to pay if they won. If the contest was fixed and the outcome predetermined, it wasn't a good strategy to have them in first place the entire time. Too suspicious. However, if they weren't the intended winners …

"They're a decoy," I said. "They've been set up as the team to beat. Meanwhile, the team the coordinators have selected to win has been hanging back safely in second or third place."

"Wait," Zoe interrupted before Zak could agree or not. "Are you saying this entire contest is fixed? Why?"

"I'm not saying the whole thing is fixed, but it makes sense in a twisted sort of way. If the sponsors have their team playing, they won't have to pay out the million dollars."

"But why have the contest at all? Do we know whether the sponsors are getting much, if anything, out of this whole event? I mean, they may be getting a bit of promotion, but even without the million-dollar prize they have to be putting out a bundle on transportation and lodging for what started out as a pool for a hundred teams."

"They must be fishing," Zak commented.

"Can you pull up the hacks for the previous rounds?" I asked. "This is the fourth place the contestants have traveled to."

"I'm sure I can, but it might take some time. It seems as if they use a new database for every level of the contest. I'll have to dig around to see what I can find."

"Wait," Zoe said. "Fishing for what?"

"I don't know yet," Zak admitted.

"Maybe they're looking for a specific hacker and hope this series of events will reveal him or her," I said.

"Or maybe they're looking for a hacker with a specific skill set and the morning hacks are tests to whittle down the potential pool," Zak added.

"Or maybe they're gathering specific data that's hidden among the contest-related hacks," Zoe said as she caught on. "Like maybe they want account numbers from a specific bank, but instead of just finding a black hat and paying them to hack into the bank, they set up this competition where most of the hacks are fake so that when the real one pops up no one will be the wiser."

I looked at Zak. "If you'd been playing this game for the past four weeks, solving fake hacks, wouldn't you know it if they suddenly substituted a real one?"

"I would, but not everyone else would," Zak answered. "The other element is the competition factor. If you're in second place, or even third, and after all these long weeks you're on the verge of winning a million dollars, would you report it if you came across a suspicious hack? Would you hesitate and not complete the hack when the grand prize was on the line? Or would you convince yourself that the bank or other site you were asked to hack into was only a fake, like all the others?"

I thought about it and realized how much of a lure the game provided. I'd only participated for a day and my goal wasn't even to win the money, yet I found I really wanted to do well the next day to pull our team out of the basement.

"So what do we do?" I asked.

No one answered right away.

"I think for now we stay the course," Zak eventually answered. "If there are real hacks on the agenda I have a feeling they'll come later in the week. If Kimmy and Kenny are decoys, I suspect they'll fall by the wayside before too long, leaving the top four or so teams in a race to the finish line. The competition will be intense at that point, but I think being fed a legitimate hack, if that's what's going on, will happen when emotions and adrenaline are high. I initially planned to hang back so as not to draw attention to our team, but now I think attention from anyone looking for someone to perform their hack could be a good thing. I say we knock it out of the park tomorrow and then regroup to see what happens."

Zoe looked at me. "I think we might want to wait to call your brother. I know figuring out what happened to Cammy is your number one priority, but getting the police involved might get whoever's behind this to pull back."

"Wouldn't that be a good thing?" I wondered.

Zak shook his head. "If there's something larger at work here—and I want to remind you both that that's purely speculation at this point—we need to figure out what it is. If we get the cops involved before whoever set this whole thing up makes their move, they'll just regroup and try again. I don't know yet what the endgame is, or even if there is one, but I have a bad feeling about this."

I agreed not to call John just yet and Zak quickly went over the other six teams in the contest, spending the most time on the ones in second, third, and fourth place because it was his opinion the true leader would be hanging back there.

Zoe announced she was going to bed, and Zak, with a worried look on his face, announced he would be turning in as well. I poured myself a glass of wine and headed out onto the lanai. It was late and totally possible Luke had already gone to bed, but I was missing him, so I took out my phone and dialed his number.

"Luke Austin," Luke answered. I could tell he was on speakerphone and, given the greeting, likely he hadn't looked at his caller ID.

"Luke?"

"Lani. I'm sorry. I'm driving and didn't look to see who was calling."

"Where are you?"

"About ten minutes from the resort."

"Resort? This resort?"

"If by *this resort* you mean the one at which you're currently staying, then yes. I'm glad you called. I was going to call you when I got there to find out what room you're in."

I paused before I replied. "Why are you here? Not that I'm not happy about it, but I thought you weren't coming until tomorrow. Didn't your mom have some sort of a party planned for today?"

"She did," Luke answered with a hint of hardness in his tone. "It's a long story, but basically, her guests turned out to be a bunch of my old girlfriends who still live near the ranch and aren't married. When I saw that her party was some sort of bizarre group date I packed up my stuff and caught the next plane to Hawaii."

I frowned. "Your mother was trying to fix you up?"

"Yes."

"So you left?"

"I did."

"Isn't she mad?"

"She is, but she'll get over it. I'm just pulling into the resort parking lot."

"We're in a cottage. Zak thought it would be more conducive to strategy sessions. I'll meet you on the sidewalk in front of the lot and show you where we are. And Luke..."

"Yeah?"

"I'm really glad you're here."

I got Luke settled into my room and went back out onto the lanai while he took a quick shower. My mood had lightened considerably the moment he walked into my arms. I could see he was exhausted and I knew we had a busy day ahead of us, so I figured I'd catch him up the best I could before we turned in.

Luke emerged from the cottage dressed in shorts and a soft tank. His hair was wet, his feet were bare, and he carried a glass of wine. He kissed me on the top of the head before sitting down on the lounge next to me.

"Do you want to talk about it?" I asked.

"Not even a tiny bit. I'd rather hear how things are going here."

I filled him in the best I could, including our current theory that there was a real hack of some sort behind everything that had been going on. It was a smart idea to hide one among a whole lot of fakes, but I wondered exactly what was at stake for someone to create such an elaborate ruse and what Cammy must have stumbled onto.

"The theory seems plausible, but have you discussed other possibilities? We've learned by trial and error that it's best not to become too myopic early on."

I leaned my head back and looked up at the millions of stars dotting the night sky. "We did discuss the possibility that one of the other contestants had pushed Cammy. Team Honu was in second place up to her accident."

"And now?"

"Dead last."

Luke put his hand in mine. He gave it a squeeze and we sat in silence for a moment before he asked about the other players and the likelihood that they might have done such a thing.

"Kenny and Kimmy Carter are in first place. Zak thinks they're being helped and most likely are only placeholders of some sort."

"Does he think they know they are?" Luke asked.

I frowned. "I suppose if they really are placeholders they could be part of the ruse, but it's also possible they have no idea what's really going on and think they're in first place legitimately."

"If what you say about their getting extra help is true they'd have to be pretty dumb not to realize what's happening."

"Maybe. They might just think they have an in or something. If Zak's right, the Carters will be eliminated around midweek. If they aren't in on it somehow, they're in for a huge disappointment. I sort of feel sorry for them."

Luke leaned over and kissed my cheek. "Who's in second place now?"

"Ivan Babikov and Irina Yelstin, the American-born offspring of Russian parents. Both are tall and physically fit and have degrees in computer-related fields. Ivan specializes in cybersecurity and Zak feels that, like him, he'd most likely be able to pick out a real hack. Irina is involved in the development of business software. They've bounced back and forth between second and third place, with fourth place being their lowest ranking. Zak isn't sure whether they'll be fed the real hack, if that's what's on the agenda. On one hand, Ivan seems to be the most likely to be successful—second only to Zak, of course—but on the other, if he isn't in on the whole thing, he's also the second likeliest to figure out what's going on. As far as Zak can tell with the limited amount of information he's gathered so far, Ivan and Irina seem to have earned their points legitimately."

"They seem like a team to keep an eye on. Were Ivan and Irina in third place at the time of Cammy's accident?"

"They must have been, unless that was when they fell into fourth. We can ask Zak tomorrow. He has a good handle on who the true contenders are. Other than Ivan and Irina, the only team he spent much time talking about is the one currently in third place. Their names are listed as Hulk and Cracker, but Zak says their real names are Steve Brown and Larry Pintner."

"Hulk and Cracker?" Luke asked.

"Hulk is this big guy, with a thick neck and huge muscles. He looks like the Incredible Hulk, only he isn't green. Cracker is the complete opposite. He's about five foot six, with shaggy dark hair, thick glasses, and a frame so skinny I doubt he weighs much more than I do. Zak says he's a legit hacker who isn't afraid to cross the line into the dark web. Zak thinks this is the team that's most likely to be selected for the real hack, if that's really what's going on."

Luke yawned as he reached his arms above his head. I could see the long day and five-hour time difference was getting to him. It was eleven o'clock Hawaii time now, which meant it was four in the morning in Texas. He must have been up for over twenty hours.

"Let's turn in," I said. "We wake up really early so we can get organized before the six a.m. email. The other four teams most likely won't be in the final mix, so there's no reason to discuss them at this point. If things change Zak can catch you up."

Luke closed his eyes. I thought he had fallen asleep, but he opened his eyes and stood up. He pulled me to my feet and then into his arms, then kissed me slowly and gently on the lips.

"I missed you," he whispered, so softly I almost missed it.

"I missed you too," I replied, wrapping my arms around his neck. "So very much."

Luke deepened the kiss, then took a step back. He took my hand and led me inside and into our room.

Chapter 6

Monday, May 1

When I awoke the next morning wrapped in Luke's arms the last thing I wanted to do was get up. A quick glance at the bedside clock informed me that it was 4:50. If I wanted to have a chance to talk strategy with Zak and Zoe and also take a shower and grab some coffee, I was going to need to get up sooner rather than later. I closed my eyes and took several deep breaths, embracing the moment, before sliding out from under Luke's weight. The poor guy was exhausted after traveling for most of the previous day.

"Lani?" he asked as I slipped a pair of shorts over my naked body.

"I'm here," I whispered. "Go back to sleep. I need to meet with the others, but I know how tired you must be."

Luke stared at me as I stood naked from the waist up. "Sleep isn't the first thing that comes to mind."

I smiled in the dark room. "There's no time for that either, unfortunately. The contest begins at six. We need to be ready."

"Okay. We can revisit the other this evening, but I'll get up now."

My breath caught in my throat as Luke flung off the covers, revealing his muscular form in the moonlit room. Damn, I'd missed him.

Realizing that my resolution not to slip back into bed was waning fast, I pulled a T-shirt over my head and went out into the common area. Zak was already at the computer, but I didn't see Zoe.

"Zoe up?" I asked.

"On the lanai."

I could see he was in the zone, so I poured myself a cup of black coffee and went through the sliding door to join my new friend. She was sitting in a lounge chair, holding a bottle of water and staring out at the sea. Her expression was serious, contemplative. She didn't even seem to notice my approach as I went over to sit down next to her.

"Beautiful morning," I said.

Zoe almost looked startled by my comment. She turned and said, "It is a lovely morning. The breeze is cool; any chance that means the daytime temperature will be a bit cooler than yesterday's heat?"

"Maybe. I did hear there's rain in the forecast. That usually cools things down a bit, although the increase in the humidity could cancel things out. I know it feels miserable when you aren't used to the heat and humidity, but you do get used to it."

Zoe just smiled.

"Luke showed up unexpectedly last night," I told her.

"He did? How nice. Did he finish up his business in Texas early?"

"It turns out he did. That means we'll have extra help today. I want to discuss things with Zak and Luke, but I was thinking maybe he could come with me today and you could stay behind with Zak. Not that you aren't welcome to come too, of course, but you look tired. Wouldn't a day of rest be welcome?"

Zoe leaned her head back against the lounge. "That does sound nice, if you're sure you don't need me. You know I'll be there if you do, but Zak plans to stay behind doing the computer thing, so a day to get acclimated might be just what I need."

Zoe had had so much energy a couple of weeks ago when Luke and I were in Ashton Falls. Her lethargy now could be the heat and humidity, which I knew she wasn't accustomed to, I just hoped it wasn't anything more than that. I knew myself it was no fun to be sick away from home.

By the time Zoe and I went inside Luke was up and talking with Zak, both looking at something on the computer screen. I poured myself a second cup of coffee, then sat down on the sofa just beyond the tables where we'd set up the computers. "Anything interesting?" I asked.

Luke turned to me. "Zak was just pointing out the various hacks the other teams were assigned yesterday. It seems odd that every team gets a different one."

"I've ranked the hacks from one to ten in order of difficulty," Zak said. "It'll be interesting to see if they appear to be randomly assigned or if there's some criteria used to determine who gets what."

"If the hacks aren't random the organizers would have a lot of control over which team ranks where on any given day," I observed.

"Agreed." Zak turned back to the computer screen and scanned the data in front of him. "One of the teams that was eliminated yesterday had been doing fairly well, but the hack they were assigned was brutal. The three hours it took them to get to the first clue set them up to come in dead last, which is exactly what happened."

"What was their ranking before yesterday?" I asked.

"Fifth, but they'd been bopping around between fifth and third all along. Prior to yesterday's debacle I would have said they had a chance of hanging around most of the week. If the competition is fixed someone seems to have wanted them gone for some reason."

"Will you be able to tell after today if the hacks are randomly assigned?" I asked.

"Two data points will give us more information than I currently have, but it will take at least three to begin to make assumptions about what might be going on. If I were to guess, I'd say we'll have a difficult hack today. I have a feeling the folks who are observing all this want to figure out how good we are. As we briefly discussed yesterday, there are two ways to approach the situation, assuming I'm correct and our hack is a tough one. I can fumble around a bit so the organizers won't be alerted to my real skill level, or I can dig in and show them what I really have."

"Don't you think they already know who you are?" Luke asked.

"I registered him as Zak Zorn," I told Luke. "Zak created a fake identity to go with the name and contact information I provided. If they become suspicious I'm sure they'll figure out who Zak really is, but we don't think it will occur to them right off the bat that a famous software developer would enter a contest even if it is for a million-dollar grand prize. And Zak has been keeping a low profile here."

"That makes sense," Luke said. "Although if you give it your all with the hacks it won't be long before they start digging around, and once they do they're going to be suspicious about your real motivation for being here."

"True," Zak acknowledged.

"Maybe just take a middle road," I suggested. "Complete the hack fast enough to give us a head start, but not so fast you arouse suspicion. At least not yet."

Zak shrugged. "Whatever you think is fine by me."

I glanced at Zoe, who was staring out the window. She really wasn't acting at all like the woman I'd met in Ashton Falls. I saw Zak noticing Zoe's faraway expression as well. He stood up, then wandered over to pause next to her. They exchanged a few words before Zoe went into the bedroom they shared.

"I guess she still isn't feeling well," Zak explained. "Maybe it's a good thing she's staying behind to rest." Zak looked at his watch. "Five minutes to showtime. Are the two of you ready to head out once we get the clue?"

I nodded. "I have my backpack and an ice chest with some water and a few snacks. We'll take the car Luke rented so you and Zoe can use my rental if you decide you want to go somewhere."

We all stiffened as the contest computer dinged, indicating we had an email. Zak opened it and clicked on the link. He took a few minutes to surf around before announcing it was a tough one, as he'd expected, but he should be able to get past the security around it in about twenty minutes. I asked him how long it would take the average good-but-not-great hacker, and he said about an hour.

We settled on having Zak get it done in forty minutes. He planned to use his false starts to try out a few theories he had and Luke and I left him to it, heading out to the little store on the resort property to pick up a few additional snacks for the day.

When exactly forty minutes had passed, Zak announced he was in. The guy really was a genius to be able to time it so precisely.

"And the clue?" I asked.

"There's a cypher, followed by an equation."

I held up my hands. "Sorry; math isn't my thing. Can you solve it?"

Zak nodded and Luke volunteered to help.

I left them to it and went out onto the lanai to call Bethany. She had texted earlier, asking me to call her as soon as I could. It was early in Seattle, so I expected whatever she wanted to talk about was important.

"Hey Bethany; it's Lani. What's up?"

"I spoke to Stone last night. At first he didn't want to talk, but I was eventually able to convince him that he needed to help if he wanted us to figure out who pushed Cammy off the cliff."

"And...?" We didn't have a lot of time; I hoped the urgency in my voice would get Bethany to the point.

"He said Cammy didn't get along with one of the other competitors, Irina. Apparently, they almost came to blows on several occasions. Stone thought they might have met at some point before the competition, but when Stone brought it up Cammy denied it."

"Why did Stone get the idea they'd met in the first place?" I asked.

"Because Cammy seemed to hate Irina on sight, and based on the looks they exchanged, the feeling was mutual. He couldn't find any reason for them to clash right off the bat, so he figured they'd brought whatever conflict they had in the past to the competition with them. And as soon as the contest began the rivalry intensified. Stone and Cammy and Irina and her partner were close enough in ranking to explain a natural competitiveness, but he can't explain that initial dislike."

"That could be relevant," I agreed. "I'll ask around to see what I can find out. Anything else?"

"Yeah. About the hacks. Stone didn't understand everything Cammy told him, but she said some of them seemed to be real. He thought Cammy was becoming increasingly paranoid as the competition moved into the final stages and although he tried to assure her the event organizers wouldn't have them hacking into real agencies or institutions, she wasn't convinced."

"Did she tell him where any of the hacks she thought might be real led?"

"She mentioned a few places early on. One was to get into the DMV to change the age on someone's driver's license and another was to hack into a bank to transfer money from one account to another."

"Money?" That seemed significant to me.

"It was only twenty dollars. Stone said he told Cammy the bank and the DMV websites must be fake, part of the game. At first she agreed he was probably right, but as the competition continued she got more and more paranoid, and toward the end she stopped sharing the hacks with him. She'd give him the clue to the race part, but she completely shut him out of the details of the hack."

There seemed to be enough evidence to support both the real-hack and the rival-as-killer theories. I knew Zak and Luke would probably have the answer to the equation any minute, so I thanked Bethany for the information and promised to call her back later.

"I spoke to Bethany," I said, as I reentered the cottage. "She was able to convince Stone to fill us in on what he knows. Stone gave her two pieces of information that might be important. The first is that Cammy may have known Irina before the competition and the second is that Cammy seemed to think at least some of the hacks were real."

"I'm going to continue looking around on my computer while you and Luke handle the morning clue," Zak said. "If some of the hacks are real we might be able to start narrowing in on a motive. As for today's clue, the cypher produced numbers that, when fed into the equation, gave us what we believe are coordinates," Luke told me.

"Great. Coordinates to where?"

Zak had a map of Maui up on the screen of one of the laptops. He pointed to a location that appeared to be near the entrance of the Iao Valley State Park.

"We can get there," I replied. "As long as we don't have to actually climb the needle, we should be in fine shape."

"I have an app on my phone that will tell us the exact coordinates of our location," Luke said. "We can use it when we get to the park and make any adjustments we need to focus in on the exact location." I looked back at Zak. "We'll text when we have the final clue."

Luke and I went out to his car and then began driving north. The valley where we were heading was lush and green and once served as the battleground for a great war between Kamehameha the Great of the big island of Hawaii and the chief of Maui. The battle was fiercely fought and so much blood was shed that it was said the water in the stream through the valley ran red. These days, the main attraction in the area was the Iao Needle, a tall, narrow mountain reaching 2250 feet above sea level. The needle was often shrouded in clouds that gave it an eerie feeling, reminding the casual visitor of the violence that once occurred in the valley below.

Luke and I caught up on the events while he was in Texas as we went. Although I was taking the competition very seriously indeed, it was nice to have a chance to chat about inconsequential things as we drove along the mostly deserted highway. Luke told me about his new niece and I shared the news of the small group of friends we hung out with back home on Oahu.

When we arrived at the parking area for the park Luke pulled into a space in the shade and we climbed out. He checked his phone, then pointed into the distance. "We need to head in that direction."

The coordinates took us to the place where most people believed the cave Chief Kaka'e once lived in total seclusion was. A large boulder called Ka Pili o Kaka'e stood in front of the cave entrance and supposedly made the chief invisible to his people. The boulder was no longer blocking the cave and few knew its current location, but the area was still considered a significant historical site.

We began to look around for the next clue. As it turned out, this one was relatively easy to find: a hand-painted wooden sign that looked as if it had been recently nailed to a tree read *Kuka'emoku holds the clue.*

"Damn," I said aloud.

"We have a problem?" Luke asked.

"Kuka'emoku is the name of the summit of the needle." I looked toward the tall peak. "It looks like we're going climbing."

The climb was steep but doable. Luckily, Luke and I both were wearing sturdy shoes and had brought plenty of sunscreen and water. I was glad Zoe wasn't with us. She was obviously fit and would normally have been able to make the climb with little problem, but she hadn't looked all that good ever since she'd arrived. Unlike the previous day, when I'd only spotted two teams during the entire day, I saw several today. The team I'd identified as Ivan and Irina were on their way back to their car as we started up the needle. I was pretty sure they'd had the easy hack of the day.

Also in front of us were Kenny and Kimmy, but only by a few minutes, and by the time we were halfway up I noticed four other people coming up behind us. In all I thought six of the remaining eight teams—including Team Honu—were at the needle at approximately the same time. I had no way of knowing if the other two were ahead of us or behind, but I wasn't going to worry about that. By my calculations, we were somewhere in the middle of the pack today; all we needed to do was stay the course. To move forward we only needed to be sure our overall ranking at the end of the day was sixth or above.

When we reached the summit we found a stone tablet with one word on it: 'Ohe'o.

"Looks like we're headed back to Hāna," I said, picturing the cool, clear water that awaited us there.

"Hāna?" Luke asked.

"'Ohe'o is the Hawaiian name of the tourist attraction known as the Seven Sacred Pools."

Luke smiled. "Did you say pools?"

I nodded. "Let's go."

Thankfully, the trip down the mountain was much easier than the one up, so it wasn't long before we were back on the road headed south.

"I wasn't aware the Seven Sacred Pools had a Hawaiian name," Luke commented.

"There are more than seven pools, depending on the water level at any given time, but the name seems to refer to a story about people being able to work their way back toward spiritual goodness by ascending from one pool to the next. The first pool, 'Akahi, symbolizes inexperience, the second, Luakapu, relates to the lifting of restrictions. The third pool, 'Ekolu, has to do with the road to perfection, the fourth, 'Eha'eha, symbolizes longing, and the fifth, Laulima, represents the removal of error through reverence. The sixth pool, 'Eono, symbolizes answering the call with a song in the heart."

"And the seventh pool?' Luke asked.

"Na Hiku represents the culmination of perfection."

"I'm impressed you remember all that," Luke said, his eyes on the narrow, winding road.

"I didn't." I held up my phone. "I remember the basic legend, but I Googled the rest."

Luke chuckled.

"What I can tell you from personal experience is that the pools are wonderful to swim in. I doubt we'll have much time, but a quick dip won't take long." I reached behind the seat and grabbed a bottle of water from the cooler. "Want one?"

Luke nodded. "So, once we get there, where do we start? I've been to the pools. They cover a large area."

I paused before I answered. Luke had a point. Unlike the two earlier clues we'd received that day, the pools were more of a general area than a specific location that could be pinpointed. Unless we could narrow things down it would take a considerable amount of time to search the entire place, especially when we didn't know exactly what we were looking for. "I don't know exactly how we're going to narrow things down, but I bet the next clue will be someplace that's easily accessible. I learned that yesterday when I broke into a church only to find what I was looking for was on a tree outside."

"The top of the needle didn't seem easily accessible to me," Luke grumbled.

"It was a difficult climb, but the clue wasn't hard to find."

"True. There are at least a few teams ahead of us," Luke pointed out. "Maybe we'll catch a break and one of the other teams will point the way."

"Maybe, although it seems unlikely."

Chapter 7

At the Seven Sacred Pools, we parked the car and then looked around. Unfortunately, we didn't see anyone else from the race. The loop trail leading between the parking lot and the pools was short, maybe a half mile, so we set out to see what we could find. The water did look inviting, even though we were supposed to be involved in a race. After a bit of discussion, we stopped at one of the pools, took off our shoes, and dove in for a quick swim. We were wearing shorts and tank tops and it was a hot day, so we knew we'd dry fast. Besides, the water felt heavenly after our climb.

I leaned back and floated on the surface of the cool water. There were a few wispy clouds, but other than that the sky was blue and clear. The scent created by the dense foliage tickled my nose and I could hear birds chattering in the distance, creating a jungle sound when combined with the many waterfalls.

After our swim we completed the loop back to the parking area. There was a sign at the entrance I hadn't noticed before. It appeared to be new, so I walked over to it. There were no words on it, just a photo of an old-fashioned airplane from the early part of the twentieth century.

"Should we head to the airport?" Luke asked.

I hesitated. A visit to the airport would fit, but the picture seemed specific. Why have a photo of such an old plane if the clue was telling us to go to a modern airport? "I don't think so. While it seems logical, it doesn't feel right."

"Do you have any other ideas?"

"What do you think of when you see this plane?"

"World War One. Fighter pilots. Snoopy."

"Snoopy?"

"From the cartoon. You know, *It's the Great Pumpkin, Charlie Brown*. Snoopy has this whole fighter-pilot fantasy going on in it."

I closed my eyes, picturing the scene from my childhood. I felt like there was a memory playing at the edge of my consciousness that I couldn't quite grab hold of. I took out my phone and Googled *WWI fighter plane* and *Maui*. There were a lot of references to WWII but not a lot of references to the earlier war. Then I cross-referenced *1920s plane* and *Maui.* "Charles Lindbergh," I said aloud. "He's buried on Maui not too far from here."

"Seems right," Luke said. "What direction?"

"Go toward Kipahulu."

Charles Lindbergh had lived on Maui at the end of his life and was buried at the Palapala Ho'omanu Church, a small building with a steeple that immediately reminded me of my unnecessary climb the day before.

"Let's try Lindbergh's grave," I suggested.

The gravesite was a raised mound with a flat headstone in the cemetery beside the church. It was a beautiful spot, with a manicured lawn and plenty of lush foliage. It didn't take long to find it. I saw two cars pull into the parking area as we looked for the clue we needed. Hopefully, the third stop was the last one, as it had been yesterday.

"We need to hurry," I whispered to Luke. "Get Zak on the line so he can log on and punch in the answer to the day's quest as soon as we figure it out."

There didn't appear to be anything obvious at the grave. Maybe the clue was in the church. The teams behind us had headed in that direction. I wanted to be sure before I abandoned the grave, so I carefully searched the entire area.

"Charles Lindbergh died in the nineteen seventies," I said aloud.

"Yeah. So?" Luke asked.

"The headstone says he died in nineteen ninety-five. The stone must be a fake."

"Who would disturb a man's final resting place for a contest?"

I ran my hand over the headstone. "I don't think the real one was removed. I think this is a fake on top of the real one. There seems to be a very thin stone set on top of another stone, which must be the real one. Tell Zak to enter 1995 in the computer."

I took a step back and held my breath. My heart pounded. If I'd guessed wrong we'd be eliminated for sure, and it would be that much harder to investigate Cammy's death and the questionable hacks. It seemed like it took forever for Zak to come back on the line.

"The code is good," I heard him say. "We were the fifth team with the correct answer."

"Is it enough?" I asked. The whole thing depended on the cumulative total of the teams below us.

"It's enough."

I let out a long, loud breath before I flung myself into Luke's arms. "Good job, partner."

"Good job to you too. Let's head back. I need a shower and some food before we settle down for our strategy session this evening."

"Let's hurry. The sooner we finish that, the sooner we can start the canoodling session."

Luke grabbed my hand and headed toward the car.

******

The sun had set by the time we returned to the resort and settled in for the evening. As we had for other meals, we ordered room service and settled onto the lanai overlooking the ocean to eat. The fact that we had made it through the first two cuts left me with a feeling of satisfaction, though I had no idea how we were going to hang in until the end of the week. Zak was holding back, which meant there was room for improvement as far as start times, but I was giving it all I had and wondered if I would be up to the challenge as the competitor pool narrowed.

"Who's still in?" Luke asked Zak after our feeding frenzy had slowed to a more reasonable pace that allowed for conversation.

"Kimmy and Kenny are still in first place, but their lead is diminishing. As with yesterday's hack, they didn't seem to be able to conquer it before it conquered itself and let them in. They actually checked in eighth today, but they had a large enough point total going in to maintain their position."

"Do you still think the plan is to eliminate them?" I asked.

Zak nodded. "They lost a lot of points today. Another bad day tomorrow and they'll fall out of first. My prediction that they'd be eliminated on Wednesday still feels right."

So far things were as I expected. I took a bite of my perfectly grilled salmon before asking Zak to continue.

"Ivan and Irina are in second—by quite a lot. I'm thinking they'll take the lead tomorrow unless something really unexpected occurs. Hulk and Cracker are in third and they seem to be holding steady in that position."

Zak paused as he took a sip of his wine. Zoe was sticking to water and salad, as she had since she'd arrived, but she seemed happy and energetic and her color had improved greatly. Maybe she'd just been jet-lagged after all.

"In fourth place is a team that's been hanging on at the back of the pack for some time. I guess they had a really good day. Their names are Trent Waller and Hallie Gold. He's the brawn and holds several gymnastics titles. He was even on the national team. Hallie's a student at MIT, studying cybercommunication. I was impressed by their credentials and was surprised they hadn't done better to this point, but it occurred to me they may have been holding back until the final lap."

"It's a sound strategy not to show all your cards until you need to," Luke agreed.

"I overheard some women talking about Trent when I went to the pool for a while this afternoon," Zoe shared. "He's not only a gymnast but competes in martial arts events as well. It sounded like he must be pretty good. I caught a glimpse of him in the lobby when they returned for the day and the guy is built. If he's been holding back he might give us a run for our money."

It sounded like the brawn half of all the other teams had a lot more going on than me. I was glad Zak had them all beat in the brains department, and Luke was really good on the fly if decisions needed to be made while we were out chasing clues.

"We're currently in fifth place and a husband-and-wife team from Nova Scotia are in sixth. Based on the information I have available the rankings will remain constant through tomorrow."

"So we're probably safe tomorrow but in big trouble on Wednesday," I stated.

"Perhaps," Zak acknowledged. "Anything can happen in a contest like this. The most physically fit team in the world can still be eliminated if they misinterpret even one of the clues. Having you on our team is a huge advantage because you know the history and geography of the area better than most. I honestly think we can hang in there as well as any other team."

I appreciated Zak's vote of confidence. I just hoped it was justified.

I took a sip of my wine before I said, "Okay, let's discuss Cammy's fall from the cliff. The competition is taking up most of my time. I wonder if staying in it is even the best tactic at this point. The contestants are all staying until the end of the week whether they're eliminated or not. Maybe it would be best to get cut so we have more time to investigate."

No one answered right away. Finally, Zak said, "There are two things going on here. One is Cammy's death and our desire to figure out exactly what happened and who to blame; the other is the reason behind her death, the suspicious hacks. I can see that being eliminated would give us more time to investigate the death, but it's very beneficial to be on the inside in terms of having access to the hacks. Can I hack in and get the information even if I'm not associated with the contest? Sure. But what I'm hoping is that whoever is behind what's going on will decide to give us the hack associated with the endgame. We'll be better able to control things if we're involved in what's going down then."

Zak's point was solid. Hanging in and seeing this through really was the best option.

"I can ask around about Cammy," Zoe volunteered. "I'm actually very good at snooping, and now that I feel better I want to have a job to do. The members of the teams who've been eliminated are bound to be bitter and I've found the bigger the grudge a person holds, the more apt they are to spill their guts."

Zak glanced at me.

"Okay," I said. "That sounds like a good plan. Zak will continue to do the computer thing, Luke and I will do the race, and Zoe will put her legendary sleuthing skills to work."

"Then I'll start with the teams who've been eliminated and are hanging out here at the resort," Zoe said. "You said Cammy and Irina had some kind of rivalry going on, but do you know if there were any participants she was close to? The contestants have been traveling together for four weeks. Rivalries had most likely formed during that time, but it also seems that teams may have established ties for one reason or another."

"I'll see if I can find out from Bethany," I offered, "but only the top ten teams came to Maui, so chances are we're more likely to find rivalries than alliances."

We went our separate ways after dinner. Zak and Zoe headed down to the beach for a walk in the moonlight and Luke and I went to the bedroom for the canoodling part of the evening. No matter how tired I was or how much was on my mind, Luke had a way of relaxing and invigorating me that I was quite certain I'd never tire of.

Chapter 8

Wednesday, May 3

By the time Wednesday rolled around there were five teams left. Kimmy and Kenny had dropped into second place and, surprisingly, first place had been taken over by Hulk and Cracker. Ivan and Irina were in third, we were in fourth, and Trent and Hallie were in fifth. The husband-and-wife team from Nova Scotia had been eliminated on Tuesday, as Zak had predicted.

The previous day Luke and I raced to Ka Iwi O Pele, where the fire goddess Pele fought with her older sister, Namakaokaha'i, goddess of the ocean. The hill and the land adjacent was, interestingly, owned by Oprah Winfrey, who we didn't run into. Once there, though, we found the next clue, which led to Wai'anaapnapa State Park, not only a beautiful spot but, thankfully, not all that far away. Eventually we were led to the Kaupo Church. I was beginning to see a pattern with churches being the final clue. It was possible the organizers were predictable in other areas too, which would provide a huge advantage to those who'd been involved in the competition from the beginning.

The hack from that morning had been the most complicated yet. It wasn't a problem for Zak, of course, but he thought it would have stumped most hackers given the false threads that seemed to be promising but ended up going nowhere. We'd decided he should aim to complete his hack coming in third. We still didn't want to call attention to ourselves, but we did want to show promise for whatever was on the horizon.

Hulk and Cracker got their hack done first, followed by Ivan and Irina. When they were in, Zak completed ours, which gave us a clue I determined led to the Nakalele Blowhole on Maui's north shore.

Luke and I chatted about the goings-on back home on Oahu as we made the trip. I asked about the horses he raised and he asked about my family. Luke and I both had parents who believed it was best to control and manipulate us to a certain extent, so I wasn't surprised when he admitted to having seven unreturned calls from his mother after I mentioned my mom had called me four times in the past twenty-four hours.

The Nakalele Blowhole was a popular tourist stop, so I wasn't surprised when we pulled into the unofficial parking area to find a bunch of other cars already there. The hike to the blowhole itself was steep and could be precarious, given the loose shale and lack of a marked path. We wore sturdy shoes, which was a good thing; the steep decline and rocks led to unsure footing.

Luke held my hand and helped me over the rough spots, and I accepted his help, even though I didn't really need it. I'd noticed Zoe usually accepted help and pampering from Zak even though I knew from the time we'd spent together when he wasn't around that she'd be fine without it too.

I had to admit I struggled with any gesture Luke presented that I felt minimized me as a person. Most women would be happy to have their significant other lend a helping hand when the path became difficult, but instead of feeling loved and cherished they made me feel defiant. My brother Jason had once commented that I hadn't changed a bit since I was four, and though I don't remember that time in my life very well, I was willing to accept it as my I-can-do-it-myself phase.

Had I somehow become developmentally stuck at the age of four?

"What now?" Luke asked as we arrived at the bottom of the hill and stood level with the blowhole, just above the sea.

"The second part of the clue said something about a turkey looking over paradise," I said as a steeple of water shot forty feet into the air.

I looked around and didn't see any turkeys, not that I expected to. I considered whether we might be after a turkey-shaped rock. The constant pounding of the sea had caused the rocks in the area to take on all sorts of interesting shapes, including a perfect heart that was frequently photographed by tourists. "It has to be a rock, but I don't see anything that looks like a turkey."

"The clue led us here, but it didn't specify whether we'd need to climb down," Luke commented. "We just assumed we needed to get as close to the blowhole as possible. Maybe we just needed to show up, and the turkey is visible from a higher elevation."

I paused to consider that. On one hand, there would be a natural assumption that a clue leading to the blowhole would require a climb down to it, but you could see it from the parking area above. There were a couple of other flat viewing points on the way down the hill, so maybe...

"I guess we can climb back up, stopping frequently to look around," I suggested.

Luke nodded to Ivan and Irina, who were at about the halfway point on the hill. They'd stopped to study a rock. After a few moments they headed back up the rock, so I assumed they'd found the turkey. The hike up the hill was more strenuous but less dangerous, so we managed to make pretty good time. By the time we made it to the spot they'd been studying they were long gone.

The fact that Ivan and Irina had been a good twenty minutes behind us and we'd completed the hack at about the same time must have meant we'd figured out the general location of the clue faster than they had. For the first time I felt we might actually have a chance to hang on in the competition to the end.

We found the turkey, then looked around for the clue. There were black rocks scattered all around, even though there weren't that many of them in the rest of the area in general, so I felt like black rock, or maybe just the color black, was a clue and mentioned it to Luke.

"Two things come immediately to mind. There's Black Sand Beach, which is popular and spiritually significant, and there's a diving rock near Ka'anapali Beach that's known as Black Rock. There are also black rocks up on the Haleakalā volcano. I'm sure there must be others in the area as well, but those are the ones that stand out to me as having both recognition and spiritual value."

"Why did you bring up the spiritual aspect?" Luke asked.

"There've been a couple of exceptions, but most of the sites we've been directed to this week have had a spiritual or at least a historical significance."

As Luke looked around, I saw Trent and Hallie had just pulled into the parking area. I figured it was prudent that we step away from the clue, so I pulled his arm, indicating that we should continue up the hill. We hadn't seen Kimmy and Kenny or Hulk and Cracker. I had no way to know for sure, but if they were ahead of us, as I suspected, Trent and Hallie were the ones to beat.

We returned to the car and discussed the obvious options. Black Rock, the diving area near Ka'anapali Beach, was believed by the ancient Hawaiians to be where, after death, spirits went to meet their ancestors. If there were no family spirits to receive them, they would wander there, attaching themselves to rocks and generally causing mischief. It was for that reason it was considered unwise to take away any rocks from the area.

Black Sand Beach, on the other hand, was on the south end of Maui, near where we'd been the day before. There were several significant historical and spiritual markers in the area as well, and in my opinion it made a good place to leave the next clue.

And then there was the volcano, which had black rocks. Haleakalā was a significant location, so I might lean toward that, but I could think of better, more specific clues leading to it that I imagined would have been used if that was where the organizers intended we should go now.

After a bit of discussion Luke and I decided to check out Black Rock, which was popular with both cliff and scuba divers, so I wasn't sure whether the next clue would be above or below the water.

"If it seems scuba diving is the way to go we'll need to rent gear," I commented. "I'm hoping if there's a dive involved it requires a free one from the top of the rocks into the ocean rather than a scuba one, which will require a lot more time and effort."

"How high off the surface of the water is this rock exactly?" Luke asked, a hint of concern in his voice.

I grinned. "Don't worry. It's not that high. Cliff divers do it all the time. I've never tried it, but I hear it's as easy as falling off a cliff."

"That's what I was afraid of."

"Are you afraid of heights?" I teased, suddenly feeling energized because I had the upper hand after all the help Luke had offered me during the climb down the cliff.

"Not heights per se, but I've seen videos of people cliff diving and I'd much prefer scuba. Unlike you, I didn't grow up in the water, and the pool near my hometown didn't even have a diving board. Not that I won't do it if we have to; I'm just saying that given the choice, a leisurely dive below the surface of the water seems preferable to a free fall from a cliff."

I smiled. You'd think it would be a turnoff that Luke was showing a weakness, but I found it comforting and even a little sexy. Not that weakness was necessarily sexy, but Luke had come to my rescue so many times I was beginning to feel inferior. That simply wouldn't do.

"Don't worry." I grinned again. "If we have to jump I'll hold your hand."

Luke winked at me. "I'm counting on it."

******

At Black Rock, we parked in the Sheraton Hotel lot. Quite a few scuba divers were there already, showing its popularity. There were signs telling people to stay off the rock, which I knew pretty much everyone ignored.

We'd discussed the situation and decided to climb to the top. If the clue was there, there was no reason to bother with renting diving equipment. I began to look around as soon as we got up there. There were fewer people around at this time of day—most jumps were made at sunset—but I figured the organizers had taken that into account. The clue would be something we could find.

To this point, figuring out the first clues had been somewhat difficult, but finding the next one after you arrived at the location was relatively easy. Everything had been left out in the open and, except for the Iao Needle, locating the clues hadn't required that much physical effort. We needed to place at least fourth today if we weren't to be eliminated.

We eventually found a sign telling us to take a leap of faith. I tried to determine if it was new or if it had been posted at some much earlier time. It didn't look completely new, as some of the others had, but not ancient either. We looked around a bit more and didn't find anything else. We needed to make up some time if we were to stay in the running, so noodling around wasn't an option.

"What do you think?" I asked Luke.

He looked over the edge. It really was a pretty decent drop. "Okay, let's do this."

I took his hand in mine, squeezed it, counted to three, and jumped. We landed smoothly in the water and then swam to the surface.

"That was fun," Luke said with a grin on his face.

"I told you it wouldn't be bad."

Luke looked around at our surroundings. "What now?"

"I saw something about halfway up on the way down. I don't know for certain if it's what we're looking for, but it didn't seem natural, sort of out of place."

"What exactly did you see?"

"A box, sort of like a mailbox but a bit smaller, and made of wood. I can't be certain, but at this point I'm willing to bet it has the next clue."

"So we climb?"

I nodded. "We climb."

The clue, once accessed, led us to yet another church. This one was close by, so if the church was the final clue of the day, as had been the case to this point, we were going to have an early day. At the car I called Zak, getting him ready to record the information, when he told me that he'd texted earlier to let us know that without help, Kimmy and Kenny hadn't solved their hack and thus were eliminated. The order in which we submitted the final information could affect our ranking, but we could take a breath and relax a bit because at the very least we'd survived to play the next day.

We determined the necessary information, Zak fed it into the computer, and we were free to head back. I suspected it was intentional that we'd been provided with easy clues, all located in close proximity to one another today, giving us time to rest. And if I was right about that I wondered what was in store for us the next day.

By the time we returned to the resort Zak was able to inform us that we were in third place, Hulk and Cracker were in first, Ivan and Ivana in second, and Trent and Hallie in fourth. To remain in the contest all we needed to do was maintain our position the next day. I had a feeling it was time to set Zak loose so Luke and I would have the lead we'd need.

Chapter 9

Luke and I took long showers after we chatted briefly with Zak. It was early still, which meant I was going to have plenty of time for sleuthing. I knew there was a lot going on, or at least there seemed to be a lot going on, but my endgame remained constant: finding Cammy's killer.

I found Zak hard at work when I returned to the common room. I grabbed a bottle of water from the kitchen, settled down on one of the sofas, and asked, "Any new insights?"

"Maybe. Based on what happened today, I think it's clear Kimmy and Kenny were plants all along. I don't know why the event coordinators chose to have them planted at the top if they weren't going to go all the way."

"Do you think there are any other plants?"

Zak hesitated. "Everyone left in the competition seems to legitimately have the skills to have made it this far, so I don't think so."

I glanced at Zoe, who had just walked in from the lanai. Her long, curly hair was pulled back in a scrunchie and she looked more than a little hot and sweaty.

"Were you taking a walk?" I asked.

"Yeah. It seems cooler today."

"The humidity has lessened, which makes the air feel less heavy. Did you hear that Kimmy and Kenny were eliminated?"

Zoe nodded. "All I can think of is that we're down to only four teams. If something's going to happen it's going to be soon. I think we need to take the time to rethink all the angles."

"Agreed. It might be a good idea to ask around, see if we can come up with anything in relation to Cammy's murder while we're at it. I'm hoping all the players will be out and about on the property. Maybe we can strike up conversations with some of them."

"You never know when someone's going to say something that will lead to the thread that unravels everything. There were only a couple of people hanging out at the pool when I stopped by. I didn't see any of the contestants who'd been eliminated, but there were two women who seemed to be on the housekeeping staff having lunch at one of the tables in the shade. I overheard one say she'd found some strange things in the room of one of the contestants."

"What sort of strange things?" I asked.

"She said she didn't know what they were, but based on her description, I think she was talking about surveillance equipment."

I narrowed my eyes. "Did she say which contestant it was?"

"No, but it was someone who was out of their room today. When the other woman said she wanted to check the stuff out the first one said it wasn't a good idea because the contest had ended early and everyone was beginning to come back."

Kimmy and Kenny hadn't solved the hack, so they probably never left the resort. That almost certainly meant the maid hadn't found the equipment in one of their rooms. That left Ivan and Irina, Hulk and Cracker, and Trent and Hallie. I had to wonder why someone in possession of surveillance equipment would just leave it laying around for a maid to find—though perhaps it hadn't been just laying around at all. Maybe the maid had been snooping while she cleaned the room. Zak had requested that we not receive maid service during our stay, and so far, he'd been around almost all the time, so having our own specialized equipment detected shouldn't be an issue. I hoped.

"I wonder what the equipment was for," I said. "If whoever it belongs to didn't take it with them maybe it wasn't being used for anything having to do with the competition."

"Or maybe it's going to be used for whatever the endgame is and this team is part of the plan."

"Yeah." I sighed. "Maybe." I leaned my head back against the sofa, settling into a more relaxed position. I let my mind drift, picturing the questions I'd been pondering written out in the clouds above me. I let my mind flow, being present for answers but not lingering on any one question for too long.

It seemed obvious to me that Cammy's accident—or murder—had been in some way orchestrated because of her involvement in the competition. I still didn't have a firm grasp on whether a shove had ended her life motivated by pure competitiveness or to keep her from revealing what she knew, but if she had been pushed I'd come around to thinking it was related to some event in her past. Stone had said there was some unspoken history between Cammy and Irina. Maybe Zak should do a search for a link of some sort between them. I wasn't sure if the answer would help us but it couldn't hurt to try.

I also wondered what Cammy had been doing by herself on the evening she'd fallen to her death. Wouldn't it have made more sense for her and Stone to have taken a stroll at the end of the day together? Stone might have been tired or they might have had a fight, but the cliff was pretty far from the resort rooms. Could Cammy have been lured there? Or had she been there to meet someone?

And then there was the endgame we'd been discussing though really could only guess at right now.

I had the entire afternoon free to snoop around; what I needed was a plan and a starting point. Zoe seemed to have picked up information by hanging around at the pool. I was hot and could use a dip, so the pool seemed to be as good a place to begin as any.

Luke was working with Zak, so Zoe and I headed out with their promise to join us as soon as they wrapped things up. Judging by the way they were tapping away on two keyboards with a singular focus, I didn't think wrapping up was anywhere on the horizon. Zoe found a table in the shade near the lap pool while I dove in. The steady rhythm of doing laps had always served as a means of helping me work through whatever was on my mind.

After I'd swum about a hundred laps I'd worked off most of my angst, so I pulled myself up onto the decking and made my way to where Zoe was chatting with a woman whose name I'd forgotten but who I recognized as being from one of the two teams cut on the first day that week.

"Lani, this is Carrie. She asked me about our being here at the eleventh hour and I explained that you and Zak were filling in for Cammy and Stone."

"I was sorry to hear about your friend," Carrie offered. "I didn't know her well, but she seemed nice. Not like some of the others, who are so competitive they'll barely even nod in your direction should you greet them in passing."

"Have you been with the competition from the beginning?" I asked as I dried my hair with a towel.

"Yes. I never thought we'd get this far. My friend Beaver asked me to join him at the last minute and I thought it would be fun."

"Beaver?" I inquired.

"He's an engineer and is always building things, hence the nickname. We can both hold our own with the computer part of the competition, but neither of us are superathletic, so I figured we'd be out in the first round, but somehow, we managed to squeak by and came to Maui as the tenth-place team. I wasn't expecting to make it out of the first round here, so I wasn't shocked when we were cut. Honestly, I'm just as glad to be out of it. There was no way we were going to win the million dollars, so getting cut early just meant we had more time to relax and enjoy the trip."

"Can you tell us how the contest went in the beginning?" I asked. "Coming in on the tail end, I'm not sure I have a feel for the whole thing."

Carrie's blue eyes sparkled with enthusiasm as she prepared to answer. "I'd be happy to. Beaver found out about the contest through a chat room frequented by high-level gamers."

"So it would seem the contest organizers were really after the hacking skills each team had," I said.

"Well, only really skilled hackers hang out in that particular chat room. I don't think geeks like Beaver are usually all that in to competitions with the word *race* right there in the title, but the million-dollar top prize attracted thousands of applicants, all of whom had to solve several online puzzles as part of their application. There were a few rounds, with fewer and fewer applicants moving forward, but eventually a hundred people were chosen to compete in the actual contest. Each finalist was required to find a partner who they felt best complemented their ability. Beaver had the brains, so he asked me to provide the brawn. Not that I can compete with a lot of the folks in this final round, but I could hold my own in the beginning."

I pulled on shorts, then settled back in a lounger. "I understand the hundred teams first competed in Boston."

"Yes. At the end of that weeklong contest there were just fifty teams left and they moved on to Chicago."

"So they cut fifty percent of the teams right off the bat?" Zoe confirmed.

Carrie shrugged. "I felt bad for the people who were cut so soon. They didn't get a lot for the five-thousand-dollar entry fee."

Okay, this was news to me. Up to this point no one had mentioned an entry fee. "So the competition in Chicago: Was that a week as well?"

"It was, and when that was over there were just twenty-five teams left. From there we went to San Francisco for week three, where we were cut down to the final ten, who were brought to Maui. According to Beaver, the hacks got a lot harder here."

I let that information sink in before I asked, "And this is the second week the teams have been on Maui. Did you compete during the first week?"

Carrie nodded. "We did, but it was for ranking going into the finals. No cuts were made until this week, but I think it was pretty clear to everyone who would still be in the running by midweek. Except for Kimmy and Kenny, who we all thought might win the whole thing, the writing was pretty much on the wall. Of course no one knew what to make of you all. Showing up the way you did had us all figuring you'd be cut on day one of this week. Who knew you'd still be in the running going into Thursday? The physical tests haven't been all that tough, so I'm assuming one of you is a master hacker."

Neither Zoe nor I answered. I sat forward, resting my arms on my knees, and looked directly at Carrie. "We think Cammy was pushed from the cliff."

"Pushed? I heard she got hammered and fell."

"Cammy didn't drink and we don't believe she fell."

Carrie looked shocked. Her face had paled and her lower lip was trembling.

"Do you have any idea who might have pushed her?" I asked.

Carrie didn't answer right away. I had a feeling she needed a moment to compose herself, and if my announcement had truly shocked her, she might need time to sort out her thoughts. Zoe reached over and placed a hand on Carrie's arm. Carrie smiled at her weakly, which seemed to help her pull herself together.

She turned to me. "Cammy didn't get along with Irina. I don't know why, but it was obvious from the beginning they weren't happy to see each other when the contestants were introduced. It looked like they mostly tried to ignore each other, but I saw them arguing a few times during the first four weeks."

"Do you have any idea what they were arguing about?" I asked.

"I didn't stop to listen. The first time I just saw them from a distance. It was the night after the opening ceremonies in Boston. I felt antsy, so I took a walk and saw them in the parking lot of the hotel where we were staying. I was too far away to make out what they were saying, but you could tell by all the arm waving and hand gestures that they were royally pissed."

"Did you see how long the fight lasted?" Zoe asked.

"Irina left. A cab pulled up and she got in. After that Cammy pulled out her phone, made a call, and then headed back into the hotel."

Combined with Stone's suggestion that Cammy and Irina had a past, this seemed like the best lead we had so far.

"And after that first time?" I asked. "You said you saw them together several times."

"I saw them again at the airport before we boarded the flight to Maui. All the teams were hanging around together, but they went off to the side and were talking softly. It was obvious based on their facial expressions and body language that they were arguing. And I saw them again the day Cammy died."

I narrowed my gaze. "Tell me about that."

"It was later in the afternoon. Everyone was back from the day's event and most of us were either eating or relaxing by the pool. Cammy had been at the pool, but she got up to go just as Irina walked up. She leaned over and whispered something in Cammy's ear, then they went off together. I watched as they walked down the path a bit and then exchanged words. Cammy threw her hands up in the air in a gesture that clearly conveyed displeasure, then headed down toward the beach."

"And Irina?" I asked.

"Ivan came up to meet her, they talked, and then went into the restaurant."

"Was that the last time you saw Cammy?" I asked.

Carrie frowned. "Yeah. I guess it was."

Chapter 10

Carrie stayed to chat with us a while longer, then excused herself when she received a text. Zoe and I were discussing the likelihood of Irina being the killer when Zoe stopped talking in midsentence and stared into the distance. I turned to see what she was looking at and my jaw dropped when I saw Cracker wearing the most ridiculous hat I'd ever seen.

It was a hard hat, the kind construction workers wore: bright yellow with a flashlight duct-taped to the very top. To one side was something that looked like a camera, and next to that was an object that may have been a small microphone. On the opposite side of the hat was a box or panel of some sort. Whatever it was, it looked high tech, and there was no way I could determine its purpose, especially from that distance.

"Do you think that's the surveillance equipment the woman from housekeeping was talking about?" Zoe asked.

"Maybe. But if he's trying to spy on someone he isn't being very stealthy."

We watched him pass the pool area and continue toward the cottages and the beach.

"I'm going to call Zak to let him know Cracker is heading his way," Zoe said. "Just because he doesn't look like he's trying to be stealthy doesn't mean it isn't meant to serve the purpose it appears to be intended for. I'd hate for Zak and Luke to be talking about something sensitive and have Cracker accidentally overhear."

I watched Cracker disappear while Zoe made her call. After she hung up we decided to head back to the cottage ourselves. Using surveillance equipment to spy on our competitors wasn't a bad idea, but I was certain we could come up with something a lot less obvious.

In the cottage, I asked Zak to see if he could find a link between Cammy and Irina online. Once he was on that I went into the bathroom to take a quick shower and to change into a clean pair of shorts and a tank. It was nice to be back at the resort earlier, making the day feel a lot less rushed. Maybe I'd see if Luke wanted to take a walk later.

Zak, Zoe, and Luke were all sitting around the dining table on the lanai when I went outside. They were discussing dinner options, but I could sense they were just waiting for me to talk about something a lot more important.

"Oh good; you're here," Luke said as I sat down next to him.

"What's up?"

"Zak found a connection between Cammy and Irina and it's a doozy," Luke informed me.

I glanced at Zak.

"It seems Cammy and Irina went to the same boarding school for gifted and talented girls when they were teenagers."

Okay, that seemed like it could be relevant.

"Both were high achievers who, judging by their school records as well as several mentions in the school newspaper, started off as friends."

"So what happened?" I asked as I accepted the bottle of water Luke offered me.

"Someone hacked into the school computer and accessed private records pertaining to both the staff and the students. The information was used to blackmail individuals for various items and favors," Zak continued.

I wrinkled my nose. "Favors?"

"Grade changes, removal of absences, upgrades in housing. Nothing too serious but serious nonetheless. Initially, the staff couldn't figure out who was behind the hack, and then one day, out of the blue, Irina turned Cammy in. Not only did she ID her as the person behind the hack but she offered proof in the form of a log she'd supposedly printed out from Cammy's personal computer."

Yikes. No wonder Cammy hated Irina. "Do you think she really did it?"

Zak shrugged. "I don't know. Apparently, the system was easy to hack into, so any of the more talented computer students could have been responsible. It was probably a group rather than an individual. What I can tell you is that Cammy was expelled and blacklisted by other top-shelf private academies. She finished out high school in a public school near her family's home."

Poor Cammy. Public school was most likely a waste for someone with her IQ. "How did you find all this out?"

"I hacked into the school's system which, even after everything that had happened, still has very weak security. I can look for more details if we decide we need them, but I don't like to be more intrusive than necessary."

Carrie had said Irina and Cammy had argued on the last afternoon of Cammy's life. Given this new information, it seemed to me that made Irina an even stronger suspect. I had no idea how I'd prove that she pushed Cammy unless there were witnesses, and I doubted there would be if they hadn't come forward before now. I wondered what the women had argued about. I didn't think Stone would know— he'd already denied it to Bethany— but maybe Ivan did. Of course he would have no reason to come clean to me. Maybe he was helping to cover up the whole thing.

"The fact that Irina and Cammy had a past is only relevant to a degree," Zoe spoke up. "Sure I can see that the argument the two had in the parking lot in Boston could have been related to what happened in high school. I can definitely see Cammy confronting Irina the first time she saw her, but the timing of the other confrontations doesn't support the revenge-from-high-school theory. By the time Cammy died, they were well into the competition and had probably gotten used to the sight of each other. It seems more likely the argument had something to do with the competition itself."

"I think Zoe's right," Luke said. "Both teams were in the top five; it seems likely they were arguing about something that had happened during the contest, or even the grand prize money."

"I wonder what Irina whispered to Cammy," Zoe mused.

"I don't suppose we'll ever know," I said. "Unless Cracker and his far-from-stealthy spyware were in the area and overheard."

"We can track him down and ask him," Zoe suggested.

"Luke and I will do it," Zak countered. "We might be able to get him to talk if we approach it hacker to hacker. Why don't you girls line up some dinner? We won't be long."

After they left, Zoe and I looked at the room service menu and ordered food to be delivered in an hour. Zoe wanted to check in at home, so I played a hunch and called my friend Shredder. As a group, we'd decided not to bring the police in yet—we really didn't have anything to give them and a law enforcement presence might alter the course of the endgame—but Shredder had once been a fed or something like it and still was connected, with the skills and intelligence that couldn't be explained any other way. He was also able to blend in when required and stay completely off the radar. If there was something big about to go down maybe he could help.

"Hey, Shredder, it's Lani," I said when he picked up the phone.

"I was wondering where you'd gone off to. We haven't spoken since the Kensington debacle. I thought maybe you were still ticked off at me."

"I am still ticked off at you, but I haven't been avoiding you. Luke and I went to the mainland for a couple of weeks and now we're on Maui. Listen, I'm calling because we're in a situation I realized might benefit from your brand of help."

I could hear him sigh through the line. "What did you get yourself into this time, Pope?"

"It isn't me exactly," I said. "I'm trying to help out a friend, but I think we may have stumbled onto something. Do you have a minute?"

"Yeah, hang on." Shredder put me on hold for about thirty seconds, then came back on the line. "Okay, what's up?"

I explained everything the best I could: that the sister of a friend had died while participating in a competition on Maui and I'd taken her place to snoop around. I told him about the strange hacks and some of the individuals involved. I also mentioned Zak and his opinion that the competition organizers were working up to something, maybe something big. I admitted I wasn't sure exactly what was going on but that we expected things to heat up beginning tomorrow.

Shredder wanted to speak to Zak about the hacks as well as the information he'd been able to dig up on the competition organizers and the event in general. Zak had been working hard since he got here but hadn't said much about what he'd found outside the parameters of the competition. I had seen him speaking intently with Luke on several occasions and suddenly wondered whether they knew more than they were saying. I told Shredder that Zak and Luke had gone off looking for a nerd wearing a hard hat but that I'd have Zak call him as soon as he returned.

Zoe walked up as I was finishing the call, offering to give Shredder Zak's cell number so he could call him directly.

Suddenly, I was feeling out of the loop, something I didn't like one little bit, and decided that when the guys got back we were going to have a serious talk about everything, including the information Zak had found from investigating the people behind the competition. I wanted specifics, whether I understood them or not.

"So the guy who wanted Zak's number; he's a friend?" Zoe asked after she hung up and we sat back down on the lanai.

"Yeah. He lives in the same condominium complex I do. He calls himself Shredder, which obviously isn't his real name. He has a mysterious past and I'm not privy to any of the details. At first I thought he might be on the run from the law, but he's saved my life more than once and I've come to learn he can be trusted and relied on."

Zoe adjusted her position "And you no longer think he's on the run?"

"No. I think he might *be* the law, or maybe he *was* the law. I'm not entirely sure, but just before we left to visit Ashton Falls he was involved in taking down a rogue FBI agent who had been killing suspects. Shredder told me he wasn't FBI or CIA, but he admitted he was *something*. My guess is that he might have worked for some sort of black ops team. He says he can't tell me the truth, and while I'm curious, I'm now comfortable with not knowing the details. I trust him, which I guess is what really matters."

Zoe nodded. "I agree. Sometimes you have to trust your gut. Your friend sounds awesome. You're lucky to have him in your life."

I chuckled. "Sometimes I want to strangle him with my bare hands, but yeah, at the end of the day, he's a really good guy to have on your side."

By the time the guys returned the food had arrived. Luke told me that they hadn't been able to track down Cracker but Shredder had called Zak while they'd been out, and after he'd explained what he'd found out, Shredder had decided to come over to Maui to help us out. He was coming in on a late flight but would be here before we turned in for the night. Zak had offered to rent a bungalow for him, but Shredder said he was fine sleeping on the sofa in the common area.

"What exactly did you find out?" I asked when we sat down to eat.

"My best guess," Zak replied, "is that the endgame for the organizers is to identify the best hackers money can buy and then trick or perhaps bribe them into hacking into something big. Based on the hacks to this point, I think it must be something with a top-of-the-line security system."

I frowned. "Like what?"

Zak shrugged. "I don't know."

"Are we sure that's the endgame?" Zoe asked.

"As sure as I can be. I came across some encrypted emails in the main system not linked to the computers the contestants were given to use. The people who sent the emails were careful not to say anything too revealing, but what was there was enough for me to get the gist of things. I think the competition will change tomorrow. There are only four teams left, and I think all the hacks will be real. The organizers are going to be interested in a couple of different things. Of course they're looking for someone with superior hacking skill, but they also want someone who seems willing to turn a blind eye to a legitimate hack in exchange for financial compensation. Shredder and I spoke briefly about the best strategy to use, but after a bit of back and forth he said he felt he needed to be here."

I hated to admit it, but I felt a lot better that Shredder was going to be here for the final phase of whatever was underway. Although I had no idea who he really was, my instinct told me he was not only one of the good guys but had connections in high places.

After dinner I decided to go for a walk. Luke was busy with Zak and Zoe had a headache and went to bed, so I had no choice but to go alone. It was a warm night with a bright moon and no clouds, so there was enough light that I didn't have to turn on my flashlight until I'd left the path running through the resort.

I hadn't intended to make another visit to the cliff where Cammy had lost her life, but somehow that's where I ended up. I guess there was a part of me that needed to understand exactly what had happened that evening. I stood on the edge of the cliff and looked down to the rocks below. The tide had come in, so the beach and most of the rocks were covered with water.

The area was completely deserted, which probably explained why there'd been no witnesses that night. If Cammy hadn't just fallen to her death she must have met someone on the cliff for some reason; perhaps they'd argued. Or she'd been alone and someone had followed her and pushed her from behind. Had they struggled? We had good reasons for not wanting the police involved yet, but a peek at the ME's report might provide us with information that could help us piece together exactly what happened.

But at some point the reason for our participation in the competition had ceased to be just a murder investigation and turned into something more.

I wrapped my arms around my waist and was about to turn around when I heard something. I paused to listen. The sound of the waves on the rocks was loud, but I was sure I'd heard something else. Something like branches breaking as someone walked on them.

I took a step away from the edge of the cliff when I heard the sound again. "Is anyone there?"

I waited, but there was no answer.

I took several steps toward the dirt path leading away from the cliff, looking around all the while for a person or maybe an animal lurking in the shrubbery. "I'm armed and dangerous," I called out as I walked slowly.

I was almost to the dirt path when something ran through the dense foliage, heading straight toward me. I braced myself for impact, suppressing a scream. At least I was far enough away from the edge that a tumble to the ground wouldn't result in a fall to the rocks below. Everything happened so fast I could hardly react, but somehow I managed to jump out of the way at the last minute and avoid the sharp tusks of the wild pig heading directly toward me.

Chapter 11

Thursday, May 4

I fell asleep waiting for Shredder. Luke must have carried me to bed because I don't remember waking up and walking into the bedroom. I reached for him, but the bed beside me was empty, so I pulled on some clothes and headed out into the common area. They were all sitting around the kitchen table, talking and drinking coffee.

"There she is." Luke smiled at me when I stumbled forth.

"What time is it?" I mumbled as I rubbed the sleep from my eyes. It was still pitch black out the window, so I knew I hadn't slept in all that long.

"Early," Luke said as he got up and greeted me. He kissed me on the cheek, then led me to an empty chair. Then he got me a cup of coffee.

"What time did you get here?" I asked Shredder.

"Not until after midnight. I needed to contact some people before I headed over. I'm glad I managed to dig up the information I did, but I'm sorry I missed your showdown with the pig."

I glared at Shredder, who had a grin on his face. "I could have been killed."

His face softened and he flicked me on the nose with his forefinger. "I know. I'm glad you're okay."

I took a sip of my coffee and let the discussion, which had to do with black hat and the dark web wash over me as I enjoyed the warmth traveling down my throat to my belly. The fact that the pig had been in the area must have been bugging me in my dreams all night. While wild pigs were common in the high country, it was rare to find one so close to a major resort. Granted, the cliff was at least a half mile down a dirt path away from the paved one servicing the resort, but it was still odd. It had occurred to me after the danger had passed and my heart had stopped pounding and I was able to breathe again, that if the pig had come after Cammy, startling her the way it had me, she may very well had jumped in reaction, falling off the cliff in the process. I really did need to get hold of the ME's report.

"Lani?" Luke asked, breaking into my thoughts.

"Hmm?"

"Zak asked you how you thought he should handle the hack today."

I looked up. "Sorry. I guess I'm not all the way awake. I'll take a shower and we can discuss a strategy when I get back."

Luke accompanied me into the bedroom. "Are you okay?" he asked.

"I'm fine. I was just thinking about Cammy. The pig charging out of the bushes scared the bejeebies out of me. When I saw it, I panicked. Without even taking time to think it through, I instinctively jumped out of the way. Thankfully, I had already walked away from the edge of the cliff, though I'd been looking at the water below only seconds earlier. It occurred to me that the same thing might have happened to Cammy, only she was standing closer to the edge and went over."

Luke furrowed his brow. "So you think her fall could have been an accident after all?"

"Maybe. Before, I couldn't picture a scenario in which she'd simply stumbled off the cliff, at least not after Bethany assured me Cammy didn't drink, but an involuntary fall after being startled? It's a theory that at least should be considered."

All this time we'd focused on Cammy noticing strange hacks. We'd assumed someone had killed her to keep her quiet. Maybe the organizers didn't even realize she'd noticed something was up. Cammy'd mentioned the hacks to Stone, but we didn't know if it went any further.

"What do you want to do now?" Luke asked after a moment.

I shrugged, feeling confused and uncertain. "I guess for now we should just continue with the competition and see where we end up. Maybe the truth about everything else will fall into place."

I took a quick shower and dressed in the clothes I planned to wear for the race, then rejoined the others in the common area. They seemed to be involved in an intense conversation regarding possible scenarios as to where the competition would take us next. Zak felt the messing-around portion had come to an end and the focus would shift from running around the island looking for clues to the hack he saw as the root of everything.

"Do we know anything about the event organizers?" Shredder asked.

Everyone looked at me. "Sort of. Actually, not really. As far as I can tell, there are three staff members who appear to be on the island to oversee things. None of them seem to be more than glorified babysitters and tour guides. They process paperwork, answer questions, and make sure everyone is as happy as possible. The posters scattered around the resort all indicate the contest is being sponsored by an online gaming magazine, but Zak already checked it out and the magazine is a front for a larger corporation called Blacker Enterprises. Luke checked into Blacker Enterprises and found out it deals with cybersecurity, but our guess is it's a front for hackers for hire."

"And the purpose of the competition?" Shredder asked.

Zak began, "The hacks all must be completed using the computer provided by the organizer. Someone is recording every keystroke and monitoring every successful as well as false move. In the elimination rounds the hacks were all fake. Since we've been here I've been monitoring everyone's hacks, and some of them are real. They aren't major, and someone with only limited experience might not even notice the real ones, but I'm sure the hackers left at this point are intelligent enough to tell the difference."

"So if I'm the event coordinator and I want to hack into a bank I use it in the game and once someone hacks in successfully I'll be left with a map to get back to it."

"Sort of. It's a bit more complicated than that, but yes, whoever is monitoring the computers is going to be left with a lot of valuable information after the game is over," Zak confirmed.

"Zak and I also discussed the fact that it may be the information we're asked to provide each day to receive the first clue that the event organizers are after," Luke added.

"What sort of information is that?" Shredder asked.

"Names, account numbers, addresses," Zak answered.

Shredder took a moment before he responded. Finally, he looked at us and posed a question: "If the people in the contest are talented enough to hack into a bank and retrieve account numbers why are the organizers even messing around with the competition? Why not just steal a million dollars?"

"We think," Luke said, "that most of the participants are law-abiding citizens who would welcome the chance to win a million dollars but would never steal it. Remember, most of the hacks really are just games and most of the contestants most likely just think the complicated hacks, like one that has them hacking into a bank, are just very sophisticated games that could be called Bank Hack. Although, as Zak said, the hackers who are still in the contest now will know the difference between a bank hack game and a real bank hack. I have to believe that those who continue will be making the decision to do so realizing full well what's going on."

"So what are we going to do?" Zoe asked.

"I guess we see what the event organizers ask us to do when we get today's email and then decide," I said.

"It should be coming through in about ten minutes," Zak told Shredder. "I'm going to run to the bathroom before what I expect to be a long and difficult hack begins."

After Zak retired to the room he shared with Zoe, I turned to Shredder. "I know you can't tell me who you are or what you do or don't do, but will you answer me one question honestly before we start?"

"If I can."

"Do you have the connections and/or authority to advise us in any sort of official way as we progress? I know you have friends in high places. Is there someone you can contact so that whatever we end up doing is sanctioned by local law enforcement or even the US government? I really don't want to see any of us arrested."

"I do have the connections you refer to and I've already alerted the ones I felt I should. My instructions were to continue to the endgame. And I'll keep those people informed as to what happens as we progress. Does that make you feel better?"

I let out a long sigh. "Much. I have a feeling whatever happens is going to be big. I don't mind a little risk, but I need to know I'm working for the good guys, not providing the bad guys with exactly what they're looking for."

Zak came back into the room a minute before the email was due to arrive. We all gathered around, knowing we'd need to work quickly when we found out where the day's hack was going to take us. At exactly six a.m. the computer dinged. Zak looked at the screen for a couple of minutes before doing anything. Then he typed in a few commands and frowned.

"What is it?" I asked.

"Camp Pendleton."

"They want you to hack into Camp Pendleton?" I asked.

Zak nodded.

"And do what?"

"Turn off the lights in one barracks, wait thirty seconds, and turn them back on."

"Do the barracks in question contain classified or sensitive information or maybe weapons?"

Zak turned so that he could look at his own computer. He began typing frantically before he paused to answer. "No. At least not on the surface. It's just a barracks that's usually reserved for visitors to the base."

I looked at Shredder.

"What about the other hacks?" Shredder asked. "You mentioned when we spoke that each team has a unique hack, that most were fake and only a few real."

Zak typed some additional commands into the computer. His brow furrowed while he worked. The people watching the keystrokes on the game computer must have realized Zak wasn't playing. We'd need to decide whether to continue in the next minute or so.

Finally, Zak spoke. "Hulk and Cracker have been asked to hack into Edwards Airforce Base. They're to access the security cameras and use them to check out the mess hall. They're supposed to report back on the color of the walls."

"Weird," I muttered.

"Are they going for it?" Luke asked.

"Yes. They never even paused. Hang on." Zak went back to the game computer and spent the next minute typing.

"Are you going in?" I asked.

"Not yet, but I don't want to pause too long either. If I try a few things out whoever's watching will just figure I'm not sure how to proceed." Then Zak turned back to his own computer. "Ivan and Irina have been asked to hack into Cannon Air Force Base and set off a fire alarm in the administration building. They too seem to be following the hack. And Trent and Hallie have been instructed to hack into Naval Air Station Fallon in Nevada. They haven't responded at all since the email was received. My gut tells me they won't. Not that I blame them." Zak looked at Shredder. "I think given the nature of the hack we should get some sort of permission to continue."

"I'll make a phone call." Shredder pulled out his phone and walked out onto the lanai.

Zak looked at me. "How well do you know this guy? He seems legit, but I can't say I'm up for hacking into a military base unless we have permission to do it."

How well *did* I know Shredder? Not all that well, really. I didn't even know his real name.

"I had a chance to work with the guy recently," Luke spoke up. "He seemed to have connections in both the FBI and CIA and he worked closely with the local police to pull off a sting that had several moving parts. I think he's the real deal, although I'm not sure exactly what his deal might be."

A couple of minutes later Shredder came back in. He handed Zak his phone. Zak took it and said hello. He listened for a minute, then hung up. He went back to his computer and looked up the public number for the NSA. He called it on the screen and asked to speak to a specific person, saying his call was expected. After providing his name, the call was put through. I could see the look of surprise on Zak's face when the person on the other end of the line said something and then hung up.

Zak hung up too and looked at Shredder with his mouth still hanging open.

"Convinced you have a go?" Shredder asked.

"Yes. Absolutely. But why did you go to all the trouble to have me call him directly?"

Shredder shrugged. "If some guy I just met told me to put my life and freedom on the line to complete a hack he assured me he had permission to complete, I can't say I'd believe him. If I were able to talk to the man in charge, and I could confirm the man was who he said he was, I figure I'd be convinced."

Zak smiled. "Thanks. I am. Now let's get to work."

Zak turned back to the competition computer and began to work with intensity. At some point Shredder and Luke joined in, using the other laptops, which Zak had jimmied so the keystrokes from the computer he was using were also being recorded on his personal laptop. Zak warned them that even at his skill level it was going to take a while to get in, so Zoe and I made breakfast, then went out on the lanai to eat it.

"Tell me about your friend," Zoe said with interest in her eyes. "Talk about mysterious. He's all blond and tanned and looks like a California beach boy, but then he gets some high-ranking official from the NSA on the phone. Zak isn't easily impressed, but I could tell that was exactly the emotion behind his slack-jawed look of amazement."

I took a sip of coffee, sat back in my chair, and crossed my legs beneath me before I began. "As I told you, I don't know that much about him. He moved into the condominium complex where I live about a year ago. He told us his name was Shredder but never elaborated beyond that. He has a dog named Riptide who adores him, and I figured any man who could demand that level of doggy adoration had to be a good guy."

"I totally agree." Zoe smiled. "My dog Charlie is my trust-o-meter when it comes to new people in my life. Charlie adored Zak way before I did. I guess I should have seen the writing on the wall. Does Shredder work or participate in any sort of income-generating activity?"

"Not that I can see. He basically just hangs out and surfs. He saved my life last June, when a wacko tried to drown me, which is when I began to look at him as something more than a beach bum. Still, most days he can be found at the beach, shredding the waves."

"Ah, I get the nickname."

"Exactly."

Zoe took a bite of the muffin she must have gotten from room service before I awoke. "When did you find out about his connection to the FBI and CIA?"

"Just before we came to Ashton Falls. It's kind of a long story, but I'll give you the condensed version." I proceeded to fill Zoe in on the adventure that had taken place just before I met her.

"I guess it's a good thing all of that happened. If it hadn't you wouldn't have known to call him in now."

Zoe was right. A month ago I might have broken down and called one of my brothers when things got dicey; it would never have occurred to me to call Shredder. I guess things really did happen for a reason.

Zoe and I continued to chat. I told her more about my family and friends and she told me more about hers. It had been two hours since Zak had dug in, which was by far the longest it had taken him to complete any other hack, but this was the US Military we were talking about. When I'd gone in for more coffee I'd overheard Zak and Shredder talking about using a back door to access the base, which could be closed after the hack was completed. That way the bad guys, which we were assuming the organizers were at this point, couldn't follow Zak's trail and access the base again at another time.

"I wonder if there even will be a race today," I said aloud to Zoe after we'd passed the two-and-a-half-hour mark.

"If there is I hope wherever they send you is close. Otherwise you might end up running around the island after dark."

I leaned back into my chair and closed my eyes. I could feel the tension in my neck. Now that we were staring down the finish line I found I couldn't wait to get to the end. All this waiting was killing me.

Luke poked his head out the door. "We got it," he said.

Chapter 12

Once Zak had turned off the electricity in the barracks and turned it back on he sent an email letting the organizers know. I assumed they had a way to verify this for themselves because a few minutes later a new email arrived on the game laptop. The clue was a riddle: *Sliding Sands descend from the place where Lilinoe covers her celestial home.*

Zak typed some words into his computer as we all stood perfectly still, letting the words penetrate our minds. Nothing jumped out right off the bat, but I was just a bit preoccupied with thoughts of hacks and where they might lead.

"Lilinoe is the goddess of mist or haze," Zak provided.

"Celestial home makes me think of heaven, or possibly space or the sky," Zoe added.

"Sliding Sands makes me think of a hill or mountain because sand would slide down from a higher location," Luke said.

"Haleakalā." I determined. "It has to be Haleakalā. I'm pretty sure there's a trailhead at the top of the summit that's referred to as the Sliding Sands Trail."

Zak typed Haleakalā into the computer. "Yep, there's a trailhead by that name near the parking area near the top."

"It'll probably be a three-hour drive at this time of day," I informed them. "We'd better get going." I was about to return to our room to get my hiking shoes but paused for a moment. "How did the other teams do?"

"Trent and Hallie didn't complete the hack nor do they seem to be working on it," Zak said. "I'm sure once they realized what was going on they decided the penalties for hacking into a military facility far outweighed the potential of winning a million dollars."

"And the others?"

"Ivan and Irina are close. I predict they'll be in within the next sixty minutes. I'm not sure what Hulk and Cracker are doing. They appear to be working on it, but they're taking an illogical path that leads me to believe they have something up their sleeves. I'm going to hack in to take a closer look at what they're doing now that we've completed our part."

"Okay, great. Maybe they aren't sure about the hack either and have decided to go in slowly to look around."

"Maybe," Zak said, but he looked less than certain.

I asked if anyone wanted to come with Luke and me, but Shredder said he had phone calls to make and people to catch up to speed, and Zoe said she planned to stay behind to do some more snooping around now that so many of the original twenty participants were out of the competition and thus more likely to be hanging out at the pool or on the beach.

Despite the fact that I was terrified about where this whole thing might lead, I was enjoying visiting with Zoe and Zak and thrilled to have so much time to spend with Luke. The treasure hunt aspect of the competition was actually a lot of fun, but something deep inside told me whatever enjoyment we'd been having was about to change into something much more serious.

The drive to Haleakalā took us past the small towns of Pukalani and Kula. It was a hot, sunny day with nary a cloud in sight, which made the cooler temperatures of the high county all that much more welcome. The landscape grew lush and green and the extra rain and abundance of open space made it a good place for farming. I was tempted to stop at one of the roadside markets that sell fresh produce, but completing the day's race before dark was going to be difficult enough without stopping.

We turned from Highway 377 onto the narrow road leading up to the national park and the summit of the volcano, and the road became very narrow as it wound its way up the mountain. The view as the road hugged the steep drop-off was truly amazing. I knew from a previous trip that bicycling down the steep road was popular, so I cautioned Luke to proceed slowly around the hairpin curves that barely provided enough room for a car, let alone a car and a bike too.

The road climbed over six thousand feet within just a few miles, which made for a noticeable drop in the already mild temperatures that can be found in towns that hug the mountainside at the base of the volcano. We drove past the first of the visitor centers and continued toward the top. When we arrived at the summit Luke found a parking spot near the Sliding Sands Trailhead and we got out to look around.

"The clue didn't actually say we needed to walk the trail," Luke pointed out. "The words *sliding sands* seemed to have more to do with the location of the volcano."

"Yeah," I reluctantly agreed. "This is a big area; there must be a way to narrow things down a bit."

Luke repeated the clue: "'Sliding Sands descend from the place where Lilinoe covers her celestial home.'"

We both considered the underlying meaning of the words.

"What about the summit, though?" I asked. "There's a second parking lot about a half mile up the road. You can get out and walk around on dirt trails that take you to the summit, as well as an observation point. Let's try that, and if there isn't anything to find we'll come back to this trail."

Luke glanced at the road in the distance. I could see the indecision in his eyes.

"I think we'll waste time hiking down this trail," I added. "So far most of the clues have been easy to find. There isn't a sign here at the trailhead, so I think the next best bet is at the summit."

"Okay. You must be correct. Hiking the trail would be time-consuming. Given the fact that we got a late start and had a long drive to the first clue, I doubt they'd have us take a long hike as well. Checking the summit sounds like the way to go."

Luke and I walked hand in hand back to the car. It was too bad we didn't have time to make the hike. I hadn't been to the area since I was a little girl, but I remembered the amazing colors and the feeling of awe I'd experienced as I made the trek with my dad and brothers.

When we reached the summit parking area we pulled into a spot at the end of a row. There were a lot of people here, but so far I hadn't seen anyone from any of the other three teams. I knew we'd solved our hack first, so chances were good the others were at least thirty minutes behind us, maybe more.

"What are those buildings over there?" Luke pointed to a compound nestled just below where we stood. There was a fence surrounding the white buildings, letting the casual observer know they weren't part of the volcano tour.

"That's the Haleakalā Observatory. It's owned by the University of Hawaii for use in studying the stars. The university also leases space to the Air Force and Las Cumbres Observatory."

I could tell, based on the look on his face, that Luke's interest was piqued. "Air Force?"

"The Air Force Maui Optical and Supercomputing Observatory is housed here. As for the observatory, the space is used to track space objects including, but not limited to, asteroids, satellites, and incoming missiles. It's also the home of a supercomputer that's among the most powerful in the world."

Luke frowned.

"Something wrong?"

Luke narrowed his eyes. "I can't know for certain, but I think I just found our endgame."

I paused, then looked down at the cluster of white buildings. "You think someone wants to break into the observatory? Why?"

"Unfortunately, I can think of any number of reasons. I think we should call Zak to tell him about the facility in case he doesn't know about it already. After that we can look for the next clue."

"Go ahead and make the call. I'm going to check out the viewing area. Meet me there."

One of the things Haleakalā was famous for, at least among tourists, were the amazing sunrises. Getting up in the middle of the night and making the long trek to catch the first rays of the new day was such a popular activity that a reservation to park in the area usually had to be made. I'd never made the trek, but I'd heard it could be a truly spiritual experience.

I reached the glass-encased building and looked around. There were perhaps a dozen people inside, looking at the displays that had been set around the room. Most of them provided information about various aspects of the mountain, including the terrain, weather, animals who made their homes here, and plants native to the area. I knew from my previous trip that the most-talked-about plant was the silversword, an odd-looking shrub with stiletto-shaped leaves and a large flower stalk. In Hawaiian, the plant is called 'ahinahina; hina means gray and the silverswood had a reputation for being sacred to the goddess Hina. There used to be thousands of the plants in the area, but now they were rare, and there were signs everywhere telling people not to touch them.

"Did you get through?" I asked Luke when he came to meet me.

"Yes. Zak thinks we might be on to something. He's been wondering since the beginning why the organizers brought the game to Maui. If the observatory is the goal, covering here makes sense."

"Okay, so what does this dummy corporation that may or may not deal in gaming want with an isolated observatory?"

I could almost see the wheels turning in Luke's head before he answered me. "I suppose there are any number of things someone might be after. The ability to view objects in space could be useful, and then there's the supercomputer thing. There are other supercomputers and other telescopes, but this observatory is pretty remote, and the security here is most likely considerably less than at other facilities. I guess all we can do is to wait to see what happens next."

"Was Shredder there when you called?"

"He was, and he's going to check in with whoever it is he reports to. I have a feeling that by the time we get back to the resort Zak and Shredder will have come up with some kind of plan."

"We should be there to help out."

Luke shook his head. "Our job is to work the race and stay in the game. We need to find the next clue and we need it fast."

I looked around. Clouds were gathering below and making their way up the mountain. I knew this phenomenon had to do with an inversion layer that was formed when temperatures clashed. The clue had said something about the place where Lilinoe covers her celestial home. There was a point about midway up the mountain where dense, turbulent clouds formed. We should probably head down to check it out. There was also a poster about the inversion layer inside the viewing building. Maybe the clue was on or around it. Finding an exact spot where clouds formed below us would be a lot more random than the placement of the other clues had been to date and Luke and I had already agreed that hiking down into the crater would take too long.

I went over to the poster that I felt best described the phenomenon with the clouds. I studied it but didn't notice any handwriting or anything that seemed to be a clue. I stood studying the poster on the wall for a moment longer, then turned and looked out the window at the incredible view. There was something nagging at the back of my mind, but I couldn't quite bring it forward.

"Have you seen anyone from any of the other teams?" I asked Luke.

"No," he said, "and that's beginning to bother me. I'm wondering if we interpreted the clue incorrectly."

"Call Zak back. Have him reference Haleakalā and Lilinoe. Maybe there's something we're missing."

Luke did as I asked and a few minutes later he received a text. Luke pulled it up and began to read. "It looks like the observatory was built on sacred ground. Over the past seventy years, construction of former and existing buildings have removed much of the physical evidence of Hawaiian traditional and cultural practices in the area, but ceremonial rocks still exist. As part of the site's long-range development plan, the area surrounding these artifacts has been set aside for religious and cultural purposes. There's a shrine that signifies it a sacred ceremonial site."

"So we need to hike down there and look around."

"It would seem," Luke agreed.

I went back outside and headed to the cliff edge that overlooked the facility. There was a paved road leading to the building, and although there was a fence around the facility, the road leading to the cluster of buildings didn't appear to be guarded in any way. We stood on the cliff for several more minutes, just watching, before deciding to go down to the road. If we were stopped we'd say we'd seen the buildings, didn't know what they were, and decided to check them out.

Amazingly, no one stopped us. We didn't need to get inside any of the buildings, which would help. Zak's text had given us a general description of the shrine, which we quickly located. Sitting on the ground in front it was a tablet that simply said *lavender*.

"There's a lavender farm not far from the intersection at the bottom of the mountain," I said. "Seems like as good a place as any to find the next clue."

"Okay. Let's go."

The farm sold everything lavender. I'd had no idea there were so many things to do with it. Apparently, you could use lavender to make chocolate, beverages, scones, coffee, candles, pillows, and a bunch of other items. We headed into the gift shop as soon as we arrived. I didn't know where to start, so I introduced myself to the woman behind the counter. When I mentioned I was with the Brains and Brawn competition she handed me an envelope, then invited me to sample some of her products.

The store smelled wonderful and I was tempted to linger, but I knew our journey wasn't yet over, so Luke and I went back to the car and opened the envelope. Inside was a single sheet of paper with a series of six numbers on it. It looked like the daily answer rather than another clue, so Luke called Zak and told him what we'd found. He typed in the numbers, then came back on the line. It seemed we'd not only solved today's puzzle but were the first team to do so.

I let out a sigh of relief. For the first time we might actually have the upper hand.

Chapter 13

It was late afternoon by the time we returned to the resort. Zak and Shredder were busy working on the computers, but Zoe was nowhere in sight. I took a quick shower before dressing in clean clothes, then went back to the common area. Luke had joined Zak and Shredder at the computers.

"What's going on?" I asked as I headed into the kitchen for something to drink.

Luke stopped what he was doing to say, "It looks like two of the four teams didn't complete the hack, so we're down to two teams in the competition."

I walked over to stand behind Luke, placing a hand on his shoulder before I spoke. "Zak knew Trent and Hallie never jumped in this morning; who else?"

"Hulk and Cracker."

I remembered they'd dived in right away that morning but at some point begun to meander in directions Zak couldn't immediately explain. "Do you think they weren't skilled enough to do what was asked of them?"

Zak shook his head. "No. Cracker could have gotten in if he wanted to, but for some reason he stopped. I'm guessing once he realized he was hacking into an actual military facility he changed his mind and bailed."

I supposed that made sense. If I didn't know the NSA was informed and we had their permission to continue, I would have bailed this morning too.

"Do you think the members of the two teams who didn't complete the hack are in any danger?" I asked.

Shredder stopped what he was doing to turn to me. "Maybe," he answered honestly. "It occurred to me that one or more members of those teams could have gone to the authorities. It's what I would have done had I been in the dark as they were, and I'm sure the event organizers know that as well. I hope everyone is okay, but I won't be surprised in the least to find that Trent and Hallie and Hulk and Cracker have been detained until the conclusion of whatever the endgame turns out to be."

"You think they could have been kidnapped?"

Shredder nodded. "Unfortunately, yes. I went by their room shortly after we realized they'd failed to complete today's hack. No one answered their door. Zoe looked around the grounds and has checked the rooms several more times, but as of the last time she went by she hadn't found a trace of any of the four contestants. I've been watching for their presence online but none of them have signed in since first thing this morning. At least not on their own computers or using their own accounts."

"Where's Zoe now?"

Zak paused and let out a long breath that sounded like a groan. "Out sleuthing of course."

"I'm going to go find her. We'll bring back some dinner in a couple of hours."

I texted Zoe, who informed me that she was on the beach near the lifeguard tower. I trotted over to join her. The lifeguard must be off duty for the day because the tower was not only deserted but locked up, but there were still people lingering on the beach and in the water.

"Congratulations on being the winning team today." Zoe grinned as she hugged me.

"Thanks to Zak, Luke and I had a huge head start." I glanced at Zoe, who had on cutoff jeans and a white tank top. "Zak said you've been out sleuthing?"

"Yeah, and I may have found something. See that man over there in the orange and brown swim trunks?"

I glanced in the direction Zoe was indicating. "That's Kenny."

"I thought he looked familiar, but I couldn't place him. Anyway, when he first came down to the beach there was another man with him. They seemed to be arguing, so I stopped to watch. After a few minutes I realized I'd seen the other man lingering around over the course of the week. Now, he could be here on vacation, but there was something about the way he presented himself that seemed off."

"What do you mean, off?"

"For one thing, he seems to be surgically attached to his phone. I've never once seen him without the thing plastered to his ear. For another, he seems to really focus his attention on whoever he's watching."

"Watching?" I asked.

"Every time I've seen him before today he's been alone. He never seemed to do anything other than talking on that phone of his and staring at people. I think he might be a private eye who's here to keep an eye on certain people. Kenny's the only person I've seen him actually interact with. Of course it isn't like I'm watching him 24/7, so who knows what he's doing when I'm not around?"

I looked up and down the beach and made a quick decision. "Let's climb the ladder to the lifeguard tower and sit in the shade. It seems as good a place as any to explore this subject in more depth. I wanted to talk to you about a couple of the others as well."

Zoe followed me up the ladder and we settled in. I was used to sitting high above the crowd and enjoyed the vantage point the tower provided.

"So about the guy you saw arguing with Kenny...did you recognize any of the other people he was watching?"

"Some of them. The ones I knew were people I'd met who were in the original ten teams but have been eliminated. He never engaged any of the individuals he watched, just stood in the shadows and yacked on his phone. I bet he works for the event organizers. It seems his job is to keep an eye on things and then report back to whoever is behind this whole thing."

"I guess it makes sense that there would be someone assigned to keep an eye on everyone. It's occurred to me on several occasions that the oversight for the contest seems to be almost nonexistent. I mean, there's an entire team helping Team Honu and not one person has said a word about it."

"Yeah. I had the same thought. It seems to me the event organizers are after something specific and the game is just a smoke screen. I doubt they plan to be around to award anyone the million dollars on Sunday."

"Agreed. Ivan and Irina are the only ones left other than us, and for all we know they could be involved in whatever's going on. If they aren't I suppose we should bring them up to speed. I have a feeling things are going to get a lot more dangerous."

"We'll talk to the guys about it when we get back."

I leaned back and rested my weight on my hands behind me. "Did you ever track down Hulk and Cracker or Trent and Hallie?"

"No. I went back to each room five times but they were always deserted."

"They could have been inside, just not answering," I pointed out.

"No, the rooms were empty. I lifted a master key from one of the housekeepers and let myself in. Trent and Hallie's room was totally empty. Not only were they not there, all their things were gone. You said the contestants were supposed to stay until the end of the competition, but it really looks as if they've split."

I frowned. "Did you notice anything else? Signs of a struggle?"

"You're thinking they were forcefully removed from their room when they refused to compete? That occurred to me too, so I looked around pretty thoroughly but didn't find anything. I checked with the front desk and they said they haven't checked out, but they're certainly gone. My bet is that when they saw the hack this morning they suspected they were in danger and went into hiding."

I didn't like the way things were unfolding one bit. "Did you break into Hulk and Cracker's room as well?"

Zoe nodded. "The place was a pigsty. There were dirty plates and empty takeout boxes everywhere. Unlike Trent and Hallie's room, theirs looked and smelled good and lived in. All their possessions, except their computer, were still in the room. It looked as if they'd just stepped out, but as far as I can tell, they haven't been back to the room all day."

I looked out over the open sea. The resort was set on a wide beach that provided the perfect backdrop for the large waves that rolled onto the shore. I tried to relax and free my mind from assumptions and preconceptions as I considered what to do next. If Trent and Hallie had gone into hiding I couldn't blame them. I had a feeling the rest of us were all in danger to a certain degree. Ivan and Irina and Team Honu had gone along with the hack and I figured that had bought us time before we were expendable, but I wasn't certain about the life expectancy of the others.

I narrowed my gaze as my eyes caught something floating on the water in the distance. "Do you see that?" I pointed to it.

"I see something, but it's too far away to make out what it is."

I wished I had my binoculars. "It may be something that fell from a boat, but I suddenly have a bad feeling. Wait here. I'll swim out to check it out."

"Okay, but be careful. If your bad feelings are anything like mine you probably aren't going to like what you find."

I didn't have on a swimsuit, but my shorts and tank were fine to swim in and didn't weigh me down much. I slipped off my flip-flops and headed into the water. I tried to hone in on the location of the object, which seemed to be drifting farther out to sea, before I put my head down and began to swim in earnest. It had been a while since I'd had the chance to take a long-distance swim and I found the steady rhythm of my strokes served to calm and focus me. I still had no idea exactly what was going on, but I knew enough to be sure that if there really was actual danger involved, it was going to rear its ugly head within the next twenty-four hours.

I stopped swimming for a while and stuck my head up out of the water to look around. The object had drifted farther out than I'd anticipated it would. There must be a strong tide in the area. I debated whether to just turn around when I realized that the some*thing* I'd seen was a some*one*. I put my head down and continued at full speed. Unfortunately, by the time I reached Hulk it was much too late to do anything other than tow his body back to the beach.

******

"Hey, John." I hugged my oldest brother when he showed up on the beach in response to my call.

"What in God's name are you doing here?"

I shrugged as nonchalantly as I could. "Vacationing." I turned toward Zoe. "This is my friend Zoe. She's visiting from the mainland."

"I'm happy to meet you," John said to her before turning back to me. "So what happened?"

"Zoe and I were sitting on the lifeguard tower talking. I noticed something floating on the water, so I decided to swim out to check it out. It was Hulk. It looks like he's been shot in the back."

John looked down at the man who was lying on the sand. "You know this man?"

"Sort of. He was a contestant in the Brains and Brawn Race taking place at the resort. I've never really spoken with him, but I know who he was."

"Do you have any idea how he ended up in the water?"

"Maybe from a boat?"

"I meant if you knew who killed him."

I hesitated. I knew the NSA didn't want to involve the local PD at this point, but I didn't want to lie to my brother either. "I don't know who killed him," I answered. That much was true. I had a feeling his death had to do with the competition, but I didn't know specifically who'd killed him.

John jotted down a few notes before asking about Luke. I didn't necessarily want John going over to the cottage and finding our command center, so I told him I'd just text Luke to come down to the beach. John questioned Luke, Zoe, and me for about thirty minutes, until the medical examiner arrived, requiring his attention. He told me that we could go but that he'd call me later, so I smiled at him and led my friends back to the cottage.

"Your brother seems nice," Zoe commented as we walked along the pathway.

"He is. He can be a bit too serious at times, but he's a good guy and we generally get along okay when he isn't treating me like a five-year-old."

"Do you see him often?"

"Yeah. My mom insists on family dinners at least once month, so I see him that often at a minimum. John isn't married and doesn't have a significant other to spend time with, so he comes over to Oahu to hang out with my brothers as well. Sometimes they let little sis tag along."

"It's really nice that you have such a close family."

I smiled. "Yeah. It really is."

Once we arrived at the cottage I went in to shower and change my clothes once again while Zoe ordered dinner and the guys gathered around the dining table on the lanai. By the time I came out they were deep into a discussion about what might have happened to Hulk and where Cracker might be. I asked Shredder if I should call John back to tell him everything we knew and suspected, but he wasn't sure. Finally, we decided Shredder would call whoever he was working with at the NSA to see what they wanted us to do.

"I feel like we should be looking for Cracker," Zoe said. "If he isn't dead already he might really be in trouble. The people behind this competition are obviously serious players with a significant agenda. If they killed Hulk and Cammy, I'm sure they won't hesitate to kill again."

"We should try to track down Trent and Hallie as well," Zak suggested. "Even if they're in hiding they may still be in danger."

Wow. Just wow. I'd come to the island to investigate the death of my friend's sister. At the time, given my past activities, it seemed a reasonable thing to do, but now not only did we have a second body, but there was at least one person missing, and we were involved in something so important that it was of interest to the NSA. I felt like I'd started off in a Nancy Drew story and ended up in a James Bond thriller. Now all we needed was a car chase and an order from our superiors to shoot to kill and we'd have completed the segue.

"Look, guys," I finally said, "we need a plan. There are too many things going on. Do we try to find out what happened to Hulk or do we look for Cracker? And if Trent and Hallie have left the resort they really could be anywhere. Chances are they're still on the island, but finding them won't be easy. And then there's the whole endgame thing we really should be on our toes about. How are we supposed to prioritize?"

Shredder stood up. "I'm going to make a call to the people I consult with. I think at this juncture we need some additional direction."

As much as I like to be in the driver's seat, letting the NSA decide what we should do sounded pretty darn good to me. In the meantime I went into the cottage and grabbed a six pack of beer. The food would be here soon and after the long day we'd had, sipping a cold one might be just the thing we all needed to take a step back and refocus our minds.

I knew the endgame we'd predicted was coming down the pike was important, but there wasn't much we could do about it until the following day. I'd come to Maui to investigate Cammy's death, but until I'd found Hulk's body I'd pretty much allowed myself to believe the wild pig had startled her from the cliff. Now I'd changed my mind again. And then there was Cracker. He might very well be dead too, but if he wasn't perhaps he'd been kidnapped and was at this very moment in grave danger. My instinct told me that if he'd been kidnapped he'd most likely still be close by. His computer wasn't in his room. Maybe Zak could track it using the device I'd often seen used to find people in the movies.

Dinner arrived shortly after Shredder and I returned to the others. We took a few minutes to distribute the food before resuming our conversation.

"According to the person I'm working with," Shredder began, "the NSA believes the competition is no longer the vehicle by which the organizers are planning to reach the endgame. As it turns out, Cracker isn't just another talented hacker. He's second only to Zak as the most talented hacker in the country. The NSA believes that when he refused to continue with the game the organizers changed course and kidnapped Cracker and his partner."

"What do they want us to do?" I asked.

"Find Cracker. The local police have been informed of his disappearance, although they haven't been filled in on everything else that's going on, and that's the way the NSA wants to keep it for now. My source also believes the people who have Cracker may have Trent and Hallie as well. It's his opinion that when they refused to play the game they were picked up immediately and taken to a predetermined location for detainment."

"Hulk probably fought back and ended up dead for his efforts," I commented.

"Hulk suffered a single gunshot wound to his back. He hadn't been in the water long. The four of them have been missing all day, so it looks like he was initially detained and later killed, probably as part of a persuasion tactic to get Cracker to cooperate."

"So what now?" I repeated.

"We're going to finish our dinner and then we're going to try to track down the others," Shredder said. "Zak will try to get a location on the missing laptops. He's been hacking into them all week, so he should be able to locate them if they're connected to the internet. Lani, you and Zoe can go back to Trent and Hallie's and Hulk and Cracker's rooms. Take another look around. Maybe there's something you missed. You didn't know Hulk was dead when you were there earlier and now that you do, maybe something will click for you. Luke," Shredder turned to look at him, "start digging around into the company behind the competition. Look for any public records, no matter how insignificant. Even an electric bill will tell us something. We'll all meet back here in two hours for an update."

"And what about you?" I asked.

"I need to see a man about a weapon. Don't worry, I won't be gone long. Once we determine what information we do and don't have access to we can come up with a plan."

Chapter 14

Zoe and I went to Trent and Hallie's room first. We figured it would be the easiest to search because it was empty. We opened and closed every drawer, looked in the closet, under the beds, and even in the shower. We were careful in our exploration but didn't find anything other than a Milky Way wrapper and a half-used bar of soap in the bathroom. We didn't find anything that would explain where they were, but we were heartened that there weren't any signs of a struggle. Maybe they really had left before anyone had the chance to detain them.

I was about to follow Zoe out of the room when, on a hunch, I went back to look in the drawer in the nightstand next to the bed. It contained a phone book and a Bible. I pulled out the phone book and opened it to the section on hotels and motels. There was a page missing. Now, I realized anyone at any time could have torn out the page, but we were dealing with missing persons, so I took a photo of the pages before and after the missing one. I figured I could find the page in the phone book in our cottage to see which properties were listed. It might be a long shot to check them out, but it was all we had.

We headed to Hulk and Cracker's room. Zoe opened a window to help us deal with the stench and set to searching for anything that might provide a clue. Unlike Trent and Hallie's room, which we'd been able to cover in just a few minutes, we were in for a long stay sorting through everything in this mess.

"Pizza and peanut butter?" Zoe said with disgust as she held up half a piece of sausage pizza covered with chunky peanut butter.

"Let's hope that's the most disgusting thing we find."

"Too late." Zoe ran to the bathroom with her hand over her mouth after finding something behind the table.

I checked it out and almost hacked myself. Someone had smeared mayonnaise on the wall and it had congealed and turned brown. At least I hoped it was mayonnaise.

I looked away before I was sick and went across the room. The two double beds, both unmade, and two bedside tables were both covered with beer and soda cans. There was something red on the sheets of one of the beds that I initially thought might be blood but was probably ketchup or maybe pizza sauce.

How could anyone live like this? They apparently had turned down maid service, as we had.

"Are you okay?" I asked Zoe when she came out of the bathroom.

"Yeah. I'm fine. The smell completely overwhelmed me when we walked in, and then when I found..." Zoe's voice trailed off, but she was beginning to look green again.

"If you want to check the closet I'll look around in here."

Zoe nodded and went there while I began opening and closing dresser drawers, which were mostly empty; most of the clothes the pair had with them appeared to be strewn across the floor. One of the drawers held a Bible, but the phone book was missing in its entirety. As with the missing page from the phone book in the other room, anyone could have taken it at any time. I doubted the housekeeping staff checked for its presence after each occupant checked out.

There was no way I was going to crawl under the bed, so I just squatted down and peeked.

A quick trip into the bathroom confirmed that Hulk and Cracker hadn't taken their toothbrushes or other toiletries. I supposed even slobs like them would take their toothbrushes if they planned to be away for a while. After opening and closing all the cabinets and looking in the bathtub, which had a black ring around it, I decided to check the rest of the room, hoping all the while my senses had adjusted to the stench.

They hadn't.

Zoe followed me, although it appeared she was holding her breath. I knew we needed to take a close look around, but there was nothing about this that was going to be anything but awful. Deciding to start near the desk, where they must have had their computer set up, I stepped over half a hamburger someone had stepped on and mashed into the carpet. Housekeeping was going to have a hell of a time getting this room ready for the next guest.

"It looks like someone took the computer but left the cord," Zoe commented.

"Yeah. They must have left in a hurry." I looked around. "If someone did kidnap them you'd think there was a struggle of some sort that someone would have overheard. There's a room above it and another below, plus rooms on either side. Why don't you start knocking on doors while I finish looking around?"

Zoe hugged me tight. "Thank you. I guess I'm still not feeling all that great."

"No problem. It seems a better use of our time to split up anyway. Meet me back here when you're done."

After Zoe left I continued my search of the disgusting space the men had shared. If someone had detained them without anyone reporting it they must have shown up with a gun, convincing them to go along quietly. The fact that they hadn't bothered to take the power cord to the laptop indicated time had been of the essence.

The sheer amount of mess and clutter was overwhelming. I had no idea what might be important and what was just part of the mess. There were items on the floor that normally wouldn't belong there, usually suggesting a struggle had occurred, but given Hulk and Cracker's casual approach to daily life who could tell? I opened every drawer and cabinet, looking for anything that might serve as a clue, but after twenty minutes I could no longer take the odors. It was just about time to check in with the others anyway.

I exited the room and looked for Zoe in both directions in the hallway. She should have been back to meet me by now. Of course if she'd checked all the rooms on either side of Hulk and Cracker's as well as the ones above and below, it could have taken her longer than I'd anticipated. I waited a few more minutes, then texted her.

She didn't reply.

I called her phone. Still no reply.

I doubted she'd go back to the cottage without me, so I knocked on the door of the room to the right of Hulk and Cracker's. One of the women I recognized from the competition answered.

"Hi. My name is Lani. I'm looking for my friend Zoe. She was going around asking about Hulk and Cracker. Is she here?"

The woman shook her head. "No. She came by maybe thirty minutes ago and told me Hulk had been found dead. She wanted to know if I'd heard anything, but my boyfriend and I got up early and went to Hāna. We just got back an hour ago. Do you know what happened to Hulk?"

"Not yet. His body was found floating in the ocean. I'm sure the event coordinators will make a statement tomorrow, and the local authorities may be by as well."

"The whole thing is so tragic. First that sweet girl falls from a cliff and then Hulk drowns."

I didn't correct the woman regarding Hulk's cause of death because I wasn't certain what was and wasn't public knowledge, so I thanked her and then knocked on the door on the other side of Hulk and Cracker's. No one answered. I texted Zoe again, then went upstairs to check the rooms.

After I'd spoken to everyone I thought Zoe would have I headed back to the cottage. Maybe she was feeling sick and had gone back without letting me know, although I sort of doubted she would have. I was halfway there when someone grabbed me from behind. I was about to scream when a large hand slammed over my mouth. I was about to try a backward kick when everything went black.

Chapter 15

When I awoke sometime later I was on a sofa in a windowless room. Zoe was sitting on the bed across from me and Cracker was sitting on a nearby chair.

"Where are we?" I asked.

"I don't know," Zoe answered. "I was walking up the stairs to the third floor when someone grabbed me from behind. The next thing I knew, I ended up here. Whoever grabbed me must have used chloroform."

I put my hand to my head. I felt a little dizzy but generally unharmed. "Yeah, the same thing happened to me." I turned to Cracker. "How long have you been here?"

"All day. Two men broke into our room this morning and kidnapped Hulk and me. They brought us here."

"Why?"

Cracker sat down next to me on the sofa and motioned for Zoe to sit on his other side. He lowered his voice to barely a whisper. "I'm pretty sure the room is bugged. I don't think they have video, but I'm certain they have audio. We need to continue to have a conversation we're comfortable with them overhearing while having a second one that's kept between us in the pauses. Do you both get that?"

We both nodded our heads.

"How's your head?" Cracker asked in a voice loud enough to be overheard.

"It hurts and I feel dizzy," I answered in an equally loud voice.

"Maybe you should lay down for a minute," Zoe added.

Then Cracker leaned in close and whispered in a voice so soft I really had to concentrate to hear him. "They wanted me to break into the Haleakalā Observatory, but I refused. Initially, they tried bribery and then minor torture, but I still refused. Eventually—" Cracker's voice broke. I was sure he was going to break down in tears, but he somehow found a way to get it together and continued. "Eventually, they told me if I didn't do it they'd kill Hulk. I didn't believe them until the guy admitted to killing Cammy. The son of a bitch confessed to luring her to the cliff and then pushing her off when she wouldn't agree to keep what she'd figured out to herself. I was stupid and made a comment about Cammy being brave to stand up for what she believed to be right and then the bastard pointed the gun at Hulk and shot him. Hulk was alive when they dragged him away. I just hope he still is."

I glanced at Zoe, who gently shook her head. She was right. There didn't seem to be an immediate need to tell Cracker his friend was dead. He was already such a mess and we needed his help to get out of there.

"Have you tried breaking out?" I whispered.

"I've been trying all day, but there are no windows and the door is both locked and solidly built."

"I could use some water," I said in a loud voice.

"The bathroom is functional," Cracker answered. "You can get a drink from the sink."

We all got up and went into the bathroom, where I turned on the water.

"What happened after they took Hulk away?" I said in a soft voice.

"I hacked into the observatory. I hoped if I did what they wanted they'd help Hulk, but I don't know what happened after they left."

"What did they want you to do once you hacked in?" I asked.

"Nothing. They said I was done for now, but they'd need my services again later."

"Is the computer you used in the room?"

"Yeah. It's on a table through the door at the back."

"We can use it to let the guys know where we are," Zoe whispered.

"No," Cracker responded. "They're monitoring every keystroke. If I deviate from the task they've assigned they'll know. I'm pretty sure they need me, but they don't need the two of you. Now that Hulk is gone I have a feeling they brought you here to serve as motivation for me to continue."

I paled. I was certain Cracker was correct. We were here to keep him motivated.

Cracker turned off the water, then motioned for us to return to the other room. "That took a while; are you okay?" he asked in a voice loud enough to be heard over the listening device.

"Yeah. I'm okay," I answered. "We need to get out of here."

This was something I'd say if I didn't know I was being monitored, so it seemed to be the next conversation to engage in for the benefit of the listeners.

"I've tried," Cracker assured me. He went on to tell me all the things he'd attempted without success. He paused several times and we continued our whispered conversation as well.

"Do you know when they might ask you to complete the next task?" I whispered.

"They didn't say. I have a feeling someone will be back soon. After the tall guy with the gun dropped you off, he mumbled something about it almost being time."

"We need to figure out a way to get a message to Zak without cluing in whoever is monitoring your keystrokes," Zoe said. "By now the guys have realized we're missing. They'll be looking for a message, but I'm not sure how to deliver it."

We continued to speak loud enough to be overheard while we gave Cracker a minute to work out a plan. Zak had been following Cracker's hacks all week. I was sure that checking his activity would be one of the first things he did when we didn't return, so by this point he knew he'd hacked into the observatory. I had to trust that Shredder and whoever he was dealing with were all over that, so I was devoting all my attention to getting the heck out of there.

Zoe rambled on as a distraction while I lowered my voice and informed Cracker that Zak had been following his hacks all week. He looked doubtful until I informed him that the Zak who had entered the contest was really Zak Zimmerman and had been on to the conspiracy from the beginning. Then his face lit up, as if for the first time he believed we all might get out of this alive.

It was too risky for Cracker to do anything on the computer until instructed to, so he used his time to work out a code he planned to implant into the pathway used for the hack. He tried to explain it, but it was too confusing for me, so I just nodded and offered my support.

About an hour after I'd been dumped in the room the man with the gun came in. He handed Cracker a burner cell that already had someone on the other end of the line. Cracker listened.

"That's not a lot of time to do it," Cracker said.

He must have been told to put the phone on speaker because that was what he did. Now we could hear the person tell

Cracker to figure it out because if he didn't, his friend would shoot us.

Cracker paled. "Okay. I'll try. But what you're asking isn't possible."

"Take the phone off speaker," the man growled.

Cracker did, and I could see his body stiffen as he listened to what he was being told. Eventually, he hung up and handed the phone to the man. Then he sat down at the computer and got to work.

All Zoe and I could do was wait. God, how I hated to wait. I knew we couldn't help Cracker; all we could do was trust him to somehow do the impossible to keep us from dying.

After at least another hour the burner cell rang. The man with the gun answered it and handed it to Cracker, who glanced in our direction before picking it up. My heart was pounding so hard I was sure the others could hear it. There didn't seem to be a way out unless Cracker was somehow able to notify Zak.

"I know. I took a wrong turn, but I found my mistake and made the adjustment," Cracker argued.

The man on the other end of the line said something that made Cracker's eyes widen. The man with the gun raised his weapon and pointed it at Zoe.

"Wait," Cracker yelled into the phone. "I've been listening to you, but now it's time to listen to me. I'll do the hack, and even though the deadline you've given me is an impossibility I'll do my best to meet it, but there will be no shooting and no more wasting of my time with phone calls. The hack you want is extremely difficult. It's going to take all my concentration. If either of my friends are hurt in any way I'm out. Do you understand?"

I couldn't hear how the man responded, but he must have agreed to Cracker's demands because he handed the phone to the gunman, who placed it in his holster.

Zoe and I both let out long breaths.

Cracker went back to work and Zoe and I went back to waiting. I could only hope the wrong turn Cracker had taken had been a message to Zak that he would receive and understand. I still wasn't sure what they wanted Cracker to hack into, but I was certain that once he accomplished his task we were all dead.

Chapter 16

Friday, May 5

I must have dozed off at some point because the next thing I knew Zoe was shaking my arm. The gunman must either be in the bathroom or he'd stepped out because I didn't see him. I heard a loud bang that sounded like a gunshot and then the door flew open. Shredder came barging in, a gun held in front of him. The man who had been watching over us came out of the bathroom with his own gun drawn. Cracker dove to the floor as he took a shot at Shredder. He missed but immediately recovered and aimed the gun at Shredder's head. I stifled a scream as the man pulled the trigger of his gun a microsecond before falling to the floor.

I did scream when a puddle of blood spread over his chest. I looked to the door to find Luke standing there with a gun in his hand. I didn't think; I simply ran into his arms and wept. Shredder was on the phone with someone and Zoe was being led into the hall by Zak, who must have been waiting outside.

"How did you know?" I asked Luke. "How did you know where to find us?"

"Zak found Cracker's hidden code."

I glanced at Cracker, who was speaking to a man I didn't recognize. "Who's that?" I asked Luke.

"Maybe NSA. I don't know for sure, but he seems to be working with Shredder. Our instructions are to get you and Zoe out of here. They're taking Cracker for debriefing."

"Shouldn't we wait until the police get here?"

Luke shook his head. "Zak's hired a private plane that's waiting to take us to Oahu. We packed up the computers and they're already loaded onboard. Shredder said none of us should be here when MPD arrives." Luke took my hand. "Come on, let's go."

I glanced at a clock on the plane after we'd boarded. It was four a.m. I must have slept a lot longer than I'd realized. Still, I couldn't wait to get home and curl up in Luke's big bed.

******

I could hear voices in the other room when I woke up. The sun was streaming through the window and the clock on the bedside table told me it was almost noon. I climbed out of bed and pulled on some clothes before wandering into the kitchen, where Luke and Zak were sitting at the table drinking coffee.

"Morning," I greeted them as I headed to the coffeemaker to pour my own cup. "Where's Zoe?"

"Still sleeping," Zak said.

"And Shredder?"

"He's busy with the NSA. He said someone will be by to interview us later in the day."

"And Cracker?"

Luke shrugged. "As far as I know, he's with Shredder. Everything that went down last night is highly classified and we aren't to say anything to anyone about our part in it. Once we're debriefed we might know more, but I doubt it."

I frowned as I sat down at the table. "So we might never know what the men who held us wanted Cracker to do?"

"I'm sure we won't be told," Zak answered. "I know it's frustrating not to know, but based on the little exposure I had to the man from the NSA I don't think we'll ever find out exactly what went on."

"But you followed the hack. You must have an idea of what Cracker was after."

Zak glanced at Luke, who held up his hand. "Zak has been sworn to secrecy. He isn't supposed to tell anyone what he knows. Not even Zoe. I'm sorry."

Talk about a letdown. I was almost killed because of that hack. At the very least I should be let in on the details about what it was I almost died for. Sometimes life wasn't fair. At least I had the answers Bethany was looking for regarding the death of her sister, although I doubted that knowing her sister died sticking up for her ideals would provide much comfort. Still, I supposed it was something.

"Are you and Zoe going to stay for a few days?" I asked Zak after deciding to call Bethany as soon as I woke up a bit.

He shook his head. "Coop," he said, referring to his private pilot, "is already here and standing by, so we're going to head home this afternoon. I'd like to come back sometime when we can relax and have a nice visit, but this trip wasn't planned and we have obligations to get back to."

"Thank you again for coming. I'm sure things would have turned out quite a bit differently if you hadn't been here."

Zak smiled. "I'm happy to help any time. That is, after all, what friends are for."

I was sorry to see the Zimmermans go. I'd only known them for a short time, but I considered them among my best friends. I was sure our paths would cross again. I'd like to spend more time in Ashton Falls and Zoe had mentioned more than once that she'd like to come back to Hawaii under more relaxing circumstances. It would be fun to show them around the island home I loved so much.

✶✶✶✶✶✶

Zak and Zoe left as soon as the debriefing was over and they were cleared to go. As Luke had warned me, we were each debriefed separately and sworn to secrecy. I'm not sure what story was fed to the Maui PD, but as far as they were concerned, none of us had been anywhere in the vicinity when everything went down. There was a part of me that would always wonder what the endgame was, but I supposed in this case I'd need to learn to live with ambiguity.

"Now that everything is mostly back to normal I feel totally deflated," I said to Luke when we were alone.

"I agree. I have so many questions. It's aggravating not to have answers for them, but in the end, I'm so happy you and Zoe weren't hurt that a little aggravation isn't that big a deal."

I sat on the sofa next to Luke, leaning into his warmth. "Shredder told me Trent and Hallie were found hiding out in a motel and are perfectly okay."

"Yeah, he mentioned it when we spoke too. It seems the NSA has determined Kimmy and Kenny were in on the plot to fix the competition but had no idea there was anything going on with the hacks. They just thought they'd been hired to create a sense of rivalry during the elimination rounds."

"And Ivan and Irina?" I asked.

"They're under investigation," Luke said. "They claim not to know about the murders or kidnappings or why the event organizers wanted access to the observatory, but they did know that the last hack they completed was illegal and did it anyway. They're in custody until everything can be sorted out. Shredder seemed to think the men behind the whole thing will all be identified and detained as well. I guess at this point all we can do is wait."

"Yeah." I sighed, continuing to feel somewhat let down.

"You have tomorrow off from your initial vacation request and you're off on Sundays and Mondays anyway. What would you like to do with all that free time?" Luke asked.

I paused to consider his question. "I think I'd just like to hang out here and relax. It'll be nice to have a few days to unwind. After everything that's happened and the frustration at the answers we didn't get, I feel all stressed."

Luke leaned over and kissed me gently on the lips. "You know what they say is good for stress..."

I wrapped my arms around his neck. "I do know. You up for a little stress relief?"

He didn't answer, just picked me up and carried me into the bedroom, where he demonstrated just how skillful he was at relaxing even the most stubborn tension away.

Coming June 1, 2017

For a preview of The Shadow scan past the recipes.

Recipes

Mauna Loa's Brandy Slush—submitted by Connie Correll

Swedish Nut Cake—submitted by Martie Peck

Chocolate Mud Pie—submitted by Vivian Shane

Butter Pecan Cake—submitted by Elizabeth Dent

Mauna Loa's Brandy Slush

Submitted by Connie Correll

Named after my mom. The story behind her name: Gramma was a schoolteacher, did a thesis on Hawaii, and fell in love with the name Mauna Loa. Gramma promised herself that her first child, boy or girl, would be thus named.

Bowl 1:
12 oz. frozen lemonade
12 oz. orange juice

Mix and let stand.

Bowl 2:
2 cups boiling water
4 black tea bags

Pour together and let stand till cool.

Bowl 3:
2 cups sugar
6 cups boiling water

Mix well and let stand till cool.

Mix all above ingredients together with 2 cups of brandy. Put in a large freezer-safe container and freeze until it forms a slush.

To serve: Put 4 tbs. slush in a glass with 7UP, 50/50, or sour. Enjoy responsibly.

Swedish Nut Cake

Submitted by Martie Peck

We have this cake for every major holiday.

2 cups sugar
2 eggs, slightly beaten
20 oz. can crushed pineapple with heavy syrup
2 tsp. baking soda
2 cups flour
1 tsp. vanilla
½ cup chopped pecans

Mix together by hand in a bowl. Pour into a greased or cooking-sprayed 9 x 13-inch pan and bake at 350 degrees for 36 minutes or until done.

Topping:

8 oz. softened cream cheese
4 oz. butter
1¾ cups powdered sugar
1 tsp. vanilla

Garnish:

½ cup whole, chopped, or pecan meal

Beat together cream cheese and butter, add vanilla and powdered sugar. Spread over still-warm cake. Garnish with pecan topping or your choice.

Chocolate Mud Pie

Submitted by Vivian Shane

My knockoff version of a dessert served at my favorite restaurant in my hometown; tastes darn close to the original to me!

1 jar (1¾ oz.) hot fudge topping, warmed
1 9" premade chocolate crust
1 qt. coffee ice cream (Breyers makes a quart size)
1 cup frozen light whip topping, thawed
1 bottle (7¼ oz.) chocolate shell topping (Smucker's)

Drizzle half of the warm fudge topping over the bottom of the pie crust. Spoon half of slightly thawed ice cream in an even layer over the fudge topping. Drizzle remaining fudge topping over ice cream and freeze for 20 minutes. Stir remaining ice cream in a large bowl and add ¼ cup whip topping, then stir in the remaining ¾ cup of whip topping. Spoon mixture over fudge-topped ice cream and freeze at least 1 hour. Drizzle the chocolate shell topping

over the pie and freeze or serve
immediately. Freeze leftovers (which you
aren't likely to have).

Butter Pecan Cake

Submitted by Elizabeth Dent

I love this cake; it's really moist and good for any function.

1 box butter pecan cake mix
1 can coconut pecan icing
4 eggs, well beaten (beat eggs before putting into mixture)
1 cup water
1 cup chopped pecans
¾ cup oil

Mix all ingredients together (including can of icing).

Pour into a well-greased bundt cake pan.

Cook for 1 hour at 350 degrees.

The Shadow Preview

Sunday, May 21

The Shadow knows.

Alyson felt a tingling at the back of her neck as a blanket of fog enveloped her in a mist so thick she was unable to see more than a few feet in any direction. She'd been jogging when the fog rolled in and was eager to get home, but the feeling of being watched was so intense that she paused to listen. The heavy air chilled her face as waves crashed onto the rocks below and a foghorn sounded in the distance. Alyson closed her eyes and listened for a footstep, a breath, or some other sign that would indicate she wasn't alone. After a moment she opened her eyes and peered into the haze. "Is someone there?"

Her question was met with silence.

Alyson looked down at her German shepherd, Tucker, who was standing at her side. She realized if there had been someone watching them Tucker would have sensed it and immediately launched into guard dog mode. She knew it wasn't a good idea to jog after dark and should have turned back sooner, but she had a lot on her mind and had found comfort in the steady rhythm of her feet pounding the pavement.

Alyson turned around and started back the way she'd come, listening all the while for something that most likely wasn't there. She'd had the sense of being watched for the past several days. She supposed it all began when she woke from a deep sleep a few nights before to the sound of whispering coming from an unseen corner of her dark room. For reasons she still didn't understand, Alyson had been able to see ghosts ever since moving to Cutter's Cove nine months ago, but this was the first time one had spoken to her. The voice had simply said, "The Shadow knows," over and over again.

The logical part of her mind told her that she was most likely being paranoid and really needed to learn to chill, while the cautious part reminded her that she *was* in witness protection and there were *real* people in the world who wanted to kill her.

Still, she reasoned, she'd been careful. There was little chance the Bonatello brothers had found her. She'd left her old life behind when her handler had arranged for her "death," as well as the "death" of her mother. He'd changed their names and overall identities and moved them across the country to a tiny town on the Oregon coast. There would be no reason for anyone to suspect that Alyson Prescott was really Amanda Parker, that the heiress to millions would be attending a public high school in a small town that barely showed up on a map.

Alyson was nearing the spot known to locals as Dead Man's Bluff on her return trip when she once again heard a sound from behind her. She paused. The heavy air was silent, yet somehow, she knew she wasn't alone.

"If there's someone out there show yourself," she demanded. "I'm not in the mood for games."

Alyson waited, but there was no response. She looked down at Tucker, who was waiting patiently beside her, and sighed. Maybe she was losing her mind. She was just about to continue when a shrill sound pierced the murky night. Alyson's heart pounded in her chest until she realized the sound was her cell phone. She pulled it out of her pocket and looked at the caller ID. It was her best friend, Mackenzie Reynolds. "Hey, Mac. What's up?"

"I'm sitting in front of your house wondering where you are," Mac said in a tone that conveyed her annoyance so well that Alyson could picture her green eyes flashing in irritation as she twisted a lock of her long red hair around her finger in a move she'd come to recognized as heralding anger or stress.

"You're at my house?" Alyson asked. She ran a hand through her long blond hair, pulling it away from her face before wiping the sweat from her brow. It was almost totally dark and the air surrounding her had cooled, but she was still hot from her run.

"We had a date," Mac reminded her.

"A date?" Alyson bent over to relieve the tightness in her thighs. She touched her hands to her feet, then just hung there, releasing the tension in her lower back.

"Just five hours ago you said, 'Hey, Mac, why don't you come over at around six so we can work on our history project?'"

"Oh, that date." Alyson stood upright and twisted from side to side. Mac's boyfriend, Eli, had moved out of town a month ago, after his father had decided to move his business back to Los Angeles, and Mac had been taking it hard. Alyson wanted to help her through this difficult time, so she was doing the best she could to keep her entertained and distracted.

"Where are you anyway?" Mac asked.

Alyson tried to peer through the fog. "I think I'm at Dead Man's Bluff. The visibility is really bad, but I can hear the echo as the wave's crash onto the rocks." Alyson squinted in an effort to see into the distance. She took several steps toward the edge of the cliff to get her bearings.

"What are you doing at Dead Man's Bluff? That's miles from your house and it's almost completely dark."

"Tucker and I decided to go for a run." Alyson jogged in place to keep warm.

"But, as I just pointed out, it's almost dark."

Alyson couldn't help but notice the tone of impatience in Mac's voice. "Yes, I'm aware of that. I guess I got distracted."

Mac let out a long breath. "Stay where you are. I'll come to get you. You really shouldn't be out by yourself after dark."

"I'm not afraid of the dark and I'm not by myself. I have Tucker. I'm perfectly safe. But a ride would be nice. It's starting to get cold."

"I should be there in a few."

"Thanks, I guess I should have been paying more attention to..." Alyson paused as her voice caught in her throat.

"Alyson? Are you still there?" Mac asked, the tone in her voice changing from irritation to worry.

"There's someone on the edge of the bluff. It looks like ... Oh God, call 911. Someone was just pushed off the cliff."

Alyson hung up her phone and ran toward the spot where she'd seen two people arguing. She looked around but couldn't find evidence of the person who had just been standing there seconds ago. She tried to make out where the body had landed below, but the fog, coupled with the fact that it had turned completely dark during the time she had been talking to Mac, prevented her from seeing the bottom.

"Hello!" she called. "Are you there? Can you hear me? I've called for help. If you're conscious just hang on."

Alyson looked at the ground around her. There was no sign of a struggle. Strange; she was sure she'd heard a couple fighting before one of the combatants threw the other off the cliff. She heard faint sirens in the distance. Mac's car pulled up seconds before three police cars and an ambulance arrived, lights flashing, sirens blaring.

"Are you okay?" Mac ran up and hugged her, two uniformed officers at her heels. "What happened?"

"I was talking to you; then I heard two people arguing. I looked toward the bluff and saw two people locked in a pretty intense physical struggle. Before I could say anything one person threw the other off the cliff. By the time I got over here whoever'd done the throwing was gone."

"Grab the climbing gear and get some spotlights on the rocks," one of the officers called to the others. Then he turned to Alyson and asked, "Is this where you were standing when you saw the incident occur?"

Alyson looked around. "No. I was over maybe ten to fifteen yards to my left, but I'm pretty sure this is where the two people were standing."

"The two of you wait in your car while we have a look," the officer instructed.

Alyson loaded Tucker in the tiny backseat of Mac's VW and climbed into the front passenger seat to wait. Someone had pulled the police vehicles up to the edge of the cliff and bright spotlights were focused on the rocks below. Then two men outfitted in climbing gear rappelled down the steep cliff face.

"I wonder who it was." Mac turned the key in the ignition and adjusted the heater to high. "The victim, I mean."

"I don't know. It was dark, so I couldn't really make out any features. It sounded like a girl and a guy arguing, though."

"Could you hear what they were saying?"

"Not really." Alyson held her hands up to the heater vent. "The whole thing happened so fast. One minute I was talking to you and the next I was watching some guy push his girlfriend over the cliff. At least that's what I think happened; I can't be completely certain. They just appeared, like by magic. I have no idea where they came from. I didn't hear a car pull up and I'm pretty sure they weren't already standing there when I ran past a few minutes before."

"But you think they were boyfriend and girlfriend?"

Alyson paused, then said, "I don't know. I'm probably just being dramatic, but something about the intensity of the moment made me think it was a lovers' quarrel. No one can make you crazier than someone you're in love with."

Mac, who had cut her curly hair into a cute bob and was dressed in jeans and a sweatshirt, glanced at the clock on the dashboard. "They've been down there quite a while. What do you think they found?"

Alyson inhaled deeply, then let out a long, slow breath. "The men who rappelled down haven't come up and I don't see an attempt to lower a stretcher, so I'm thinking a dead body."

Mac took Alyson's hand in hers. "I hate to say it, but I'm afraid you're right. It's a pretty good drop to down. I don't see how anyone could survive it."

Alyson felt a tear at the corner of her eye as she tried to still her pounding heart. She'd only moved to Cutter's Cove the previous August, so she didn't know a lot of the people who lived there, other than the kids who attended the high school she did, so she most likely wouldn't know the victim, but the thought that someone had just died left her feeling sad and uncertain. "Why do they call this Dead

Man's Bluff anyway? Have other people died here?"

"I don't know." Mac reached across Alyson and opened the glove box. "I never thought about it before." She pulled out a pair of gym socks and handed them to her shivering friend. "Here, put these on; your feet must be soaked."

"Thanks. I guess I didn't take into account the amount of mud last night's rain would have caused when I decided to jog along the shoreline trail." Alyson peeled off her previously white Nikes and damp sport socks and rolled Mac's offering onto her feet.

"So you didn't notice the people before you saw one of them being pushed from the edge?" Mac slid a stick of gum from the pack she found on the dashboard and offered another to Alyson.

Alyson folded the gum into her mouth. "No. It was so strange. One minute I was talking to you and the next they just appeared."

"What do you mean, appeared?" Mac adjusted the air vents so the side windows would defrost.

"I didn't see them the whole time I was talking to you and then poof, there they were." Alyson glanced at the emergency response team. "It looks like they're packing up."

The ambulance and a couple of police cars pulled away. The officer who had spoken to them walked toward Mac's car. Alyson opened the door and got out. "What'd you find?"

Books by Kathi Daley

Come for the murder, stay for the romance.

Zoe Donovan Cozy Mystery:

Halloween Hijinks
The Trouble With Turkeys
Christmas Crazy
Cupid's Curse
Big Bunny Bump-off
Beach Blanket Barbie
Maui Madness
Derby Divas
Haunted Hamlet
Turkeys, Tuxes, and Tabbies
Christmas Cozy
Alaskan Alliance
Matrimony Meltdown
Soul Surrender
Heavenly Honeymoon
Hopscotch Homicide
Ghostly Graveyard
Santa Sleuth
Shamrock Shenanigans
Kitten Kaboodle
Costume Catastrophe
Candy Cane Caper

Holiday Hangover
Easter Escapade
Camp Carter – *July 2017*

Zimmerman Academy The New Normal
Ashton Falls Cozy Cookbook

Tj Jensen Paradise Lake Mysteries by Henery Press
Pumpkins in Paradise
Snowmen in Paradise
Bikinis in Paradise
Christmas in Paradise
Puppies in Paradise
Halloween in Paradise
Treasure in Paradise
Fireworks in Paradise – *October 2017*

Whales and Tails Cozy Mystery:
Romeow and Juliet
The Mad Catter
Grimm's Furry Tail
Much Ado About Felines
Legend of Tabby Hollow
Cat of Christmas Past
A Tale of Two Tabbies
The Great Catsby
Count Catula
The Cat of Christmas Present
A Winter's Tail
The Taming of the Tabby – *June 2017*

Seacliff High Mystery:
The Secret
The Curse
The Relic
The Conspiracy
The Grudge

Sand and Sea Hawaiian Mystery:
Murder at Dolphin Bay
Murder at Sunrise Beach
Murder at the Witching Hour
Murder at Christmas

Murder at Turtle Cove
Murder at Waters Edge

Road to Christmas Romance:
Road to Christmas Past

Writer's Retreat Southern Mystery:
First Case
Second Look – *July 2017*

Kathi Daley lives with her husband, kids, grandkids, and Bernese mountain dogs in beautiful Lake Tahoe. When she isn't writing, she likes to read (preferably at the beach or by the fire), cook (preferably something with chocolate or cheese), and garden (planting and planning, not weeding). She also enjoys spending time on the water when she's not hiking, biking, or snowshoeing the miles of desolate trails surrounding her home.

Kathi uses the mountain setting in which she lives, along with the animals (wild and domestic) that share her home, as inspiration for her cozy mysteries.

Kathi is a top 100 mystery writer for Amazon and won the 2014 award for both Best Cozy Mystery Author and Best Cozy Mystery Series.

She currently writes six series: Zoe Donovan Cozy Mysteries, Whales and Tails Island Mysteries, Sand and Sea Hawaiian Mysteries, Tj Jensen Paradise Lake Mysteries, Writer's Retreat Southern Mysteries, and Seacliff High Teen Mysteries.

Giveaway:

I do a giveaway for books, swag, and gift cards every week in my newsletter, *The Daley Weekly*
http://eepurl.com/NRPDf

Other links to check out:
Kathi Daley Blog – publishes each Friday
http://kathidaleyblog.com
Webpage – **www.kathidaley.com**
Facebook at Kathi Daley Books –
www.facebook.com/kathidaleybooks
Kathi Daley Teen –
www.facebook.com/kathidaleyteen
Kathi Daley Books Group Page –
https://www.facebook.com/groups/569578823146850/
E-mail – **kathidaley@kathidaley.com**
Goodreads –
https://www.goodreads.com/author/show/7278377.Kathi_Daley
Twitter at Kathi Daley@kathidaley –
https://twitter.com/kathidaley
Amazon Author Page –
https://www.amazon.com/author/kathidaley

BookBub –
**https://www.bookbub.com/authors/
kathi-daley**
Pinterest –
**http://www.pinterest.com/kathidale
y/**